Nobody's Garden

Nobody's Garden

BY CORDELIA JONES

Illustrated by Victor Ambrus

Charles Scribner's Sons *New York*

A – 3.66 [UJ]

Printed in the United States of America
Library of Congress Catalog Card Number 66-18183

CONTENTS

Nobody's Garden

ONE

Hilary asks Herself out to Tea

Hilary Toft was a tactless child, and one who never stopped talking. Her name was a byword among those who knew her—her teachers, relations, and friends of the family—who would exclaim with surprise, "And yet her mother is so nice!" For the contrast with Mrs. Toft, so quiet and tactful and understanding, made Hilary's prime fault all the more obvious. She had one habit in particular that she was famous for, which her mother called "asking herself out to tea." Hilary would always assert that she never went without invitation, yet it was surprising how often she would turn up after school at a friend's house and receive an impromptu "invitation." This was very remarkable since, at this time, just after the Second World War, food was still rationed and teaparties were not often held.

So Mrs. Toft was not surprised when her daughter failed to arrive home to tea on the first day of term. Later in the evening Hilary came in and dumped her satchel in the hall. Mrs. Toft came out of the drawing room and said: "I suppose you've had your tea?"

"I was asked," said Hilary hastily. Her mother looked at her doubtfully.

"I was, really. I say, there's a new girl in our class. She's ever so queer. She never says anything. It's all right, isn't it, 'cos I've asked her back to tea here on Friday? She can come, can't she?"

"You don't mean to say that you asked yourself to tea with a new girl who doesn't even know you?"

"Yes. I mean, I didn't ask myself. Her aunt invited me. She really did."

"I suppose you had already come into the house and were sitting down to the tea table by then."

"No, I wasn't, Mummy. I was standing in the street, just going to go away, when this Mrs. Sanders said to Bridget, that's the new girl, 'Why don't you ask your friend to come in?' And when I got in, she said, the aunt, that is, 'I hope you can stay to tea.' "

Mrs. Toft frowned. It seemed a most unlikely story. "Are you sure that's what she said?"

"Um," said Hilary, thinking. "No. She said, 'Would your mother mind if you stayed to tea?' "

It sounded circumstantial. "She must be a very queer woman," said Mrs. Toft.

"And Bridget can come to tea on Friday?"

"Yes, certainly, I suppose so. You say she lives with her aunt?"

"Yes. Her mother and father were both killed in the

War. Miss Hammond said we must all be specially kind to her because of that. That's why I asked her to tea."

This is what had happened. After prayers Miss Hammond announced, "We are to have a new girl this term. Miss Mills"—who was the headmistress—"will be bringing her round presently, and you must all make an effort to be kind to her, as she has lost both her parents in the War. And we want her to settle down and be happy here, don't we?" All the girls were surprised; not because there was to be a new girl—there had been plenty before—but because none before had ever merited any special introduction. They had just appeared and been left to sink or swim. Then why should this one be so different? That she was an orphan was not sufficient explanation.

Presently Miss Mills appeared. Everyone rose.

"I hope I'm not disturbing you, Miss Hammond," she said. "Sit down, girls. This is Bridget Sanders."

The girl at her side was rather thin; her dun-colored hair was cut short and combed very neat and smooth; her face was the color of underbaked pastry. Everyone stared at her. But she did not return their interest; she stared straight in front of her, seeming not to see them. She might have been looking at the map at the back of the classroom, but she did not seem to see even that.

"Now, let me see," said Miss Mills, her eye roving round the class. "Ah! Catherine Newland."

"Yes, Miss Mills."

"Now, Catherine, will you take charge of Bridget and look after her?"

Catherine came forward, a smile ready. But there was no returning smile. When Catherine spoke, the new girl drew her head back suddenly, as if expecting a slap, and then dropped her eyes to the floorboards.

"I'm sure she'll settle down quickly," said Miss Mills to Miss Hammond. But there was a look of doubt in her face. Then she went.

At the moment when the headmistress's eye had gone roving round the class, a good many girls had each hoped that it would light upon herself. Hilary was amongst this number, for she was a girl who was slow to realize what other people thought of her. In fact, Miss Mills did not glance at her; she thought she would be a most unsuitable guardian for a shy and lonely girl.

Hilary was not really disappointed that she had not been chosen. She intended, anyway, to adopt the new girl; if she had not got official recognition, she would do it all the same. At recess she introduced herself. At lunch she secured herself a place next to Bridget. And at the end of the afternoon she left the school building in the company of Catherine and her ward.

The three of them walked down Holland Park Avenue together, the new girl in the middle, with Catherine on one side walking demurely, and on the other Hilary, gesticulating and talking and not looking where she was going. Bridget walked on, unseeing and unhearing, apparently, with a pinched look of misery on her thin face. Of this Hilary took no notice, but rattled on, oblivious of her audience. Catherine listened politely, but presently she stopped and, breaking into the conversation, said, "I turn off here. See you tomorrow, Bridget. And you, Hilary."

She crossed the road and turned up Holland Walk, as she lived in one of the streets on the far slopes of Campden Hill. Hilary was left with the new girl in her clutches. They stood for a moment on the pavement, Bridget not quite sure how to make her escape, and Hilary looking her up and down speculatively.

Then, "Where do you live?" she asked.

The new girl was startled at being asked a question. She drew back her head and then said very quickly: "In Banbury Terrace."

"Oh, good," said Hilary cheerfully, setting off once

more down the road, " 'cos I live in Hereford Villas, so I can go home by way of you." Anyone who knows that part of London will know that she was going considerably out of her way; but Bridget was a stranger there and could only submit in silence.

As they walked along Hilary began to interrogate her companion. How long had she lived here? She had to repeat her question, and when Bridget realized an answer was required of her she blenched and replied abruptly: "A fortnight."

But she had lived in London before? "No."

"Ah then, you won't know this part of the world?" If Hilary had meant this as a question she got no answer, so on she went. "Of course, I know it as well as the back of my own hand. I was born in the same house in Hereford Villas where we lived all through the War, and we live there still." Next she asked Bridget whether she had visited Kensington Gardens. There was no answer at first, so she repeated her question. Had she been to Kensington Gardens?

"No."

Or the Portobello Market?

"No."

Hilary was glad. She would be able to take her round and show her what was to be seen in the neighborhood. As she chattered on, they turned a corner and started to walk down Banbury Terrace.

The houses in Banbury Terrace were stucco-fronted, as is common in that part of London. They were very dilapidated in appearance, for stucco must be constantly

repainted, and during the War it had been impossible to do this; so the houses were black with grime, seamed with cracks, and coming out into unsightly blisters rather like chicken pox. One or two, which had been repainted since the end of the War, looked remarkably clean and smart in contrast. Bridget's house was one of these.

There was a light on in the basement window, and a woman ironing inside. Bridget looked at Hilary in a bewildered manner, as if not knowing how to get rid of her, and then hurried down the area steps, like a rabbit scuttling off. As she reached the bottom, the basement door opened and the ironing woman appeared, all smiles.

"Had a good day? Like your new school?" she asked cheerfully, and then, looking up at Hilary, who was still standing on the pavement above, she added, "Made a little friend already? Ask her to come in."

Although Bridget did not endorse the invitation, Hilary accepted it with alacrity, and came down the area steps.

"Your mother won't mind if you stay to tea?" the lady said. "I'm so glad Bridget has found herself a friend."

"It's very kind of you," said Hilary. "Mummy won't mind at all, I'm sure."

The lady ushered them into the kitchen at the back, where tea was spread on the table. Then she introduced herself: "I'm Mrs. Sanders, Bridget's aunt."

So Hilary introduced herself and was introduced to Robin, Mrs. Sander's little boy, who now came running into the kitchen. He was about four years old. Then they all sat down round the table to bread and margarine and jam.

Mrs. Sanders apologized for the margarine. "I'm afraid

we've always run through the butter ration by this time of the week."

Then, when she had finished pouring out tea, she asked if Hilary lived nearby. Hilary explained. She added, "And Bridget was saying she had only been a fortnight in London, so she's quite a newcomer."

"Yes, that's it. She came here just after Christmas. She was living with my sister-in-law in Surrey before, so she has no friends here. I hope she will soon make some and settle down happily."

They both looked at Bridget, who continued eating her bread and jam without looking up. She seemed to be completely unaware that they were talking about her or trying to talk to her. Mrs. Sanders frowned, and rose to fetch the kettle. Bridget's uncommunicativeness got on her nerves.

Hilary did not really feel surprised that she had been asked in to tea. It was not until her mother pointed it out to her that she realized it was a little odd. But the fact was that Mrs. Sanders was only too pleased to find that another child had paired off with this strange silent niece of her husband's. A friend, she hoped, would make her more normal.

While Mrs. Sanders poured out second cups of tea, Hilary began to hold forth on one of her favorite subjects—London in the War.

"London got so empty then," she said. "I remember once we went to Kew for my birthday; let's see, it would be my ninth birthday, I think. That would be in 1944, in July."

"Why you're almost of an age with Bridget," interrupted Mrs. Sanders. "She's twelve too, now, and her birthday's in August." They both smiled across at Bridget, who flinched slightly on finding herself the center of attention. So Hilary plunged on. "As I was saying, we went to Kew. It was a Sunday, the most marvellous day you could imagine. They had been making hay in the wild parts, and do you know, we spent the whole day there without seeing anybody at all! There was absolutely nobody there! I felt as if the place was ours. It felt rather mysterious, as if it were a secret place, and nobody else ever went there. It's not like that now—last summer we were there and it was crowded, absolutely crowded, and it wasn't a very nice day, either."

When they had finished eating, there was a lull in the conversation, a lull in which both Hilary and Mrs. Sanders became aware that Bridget was still there and still silent. Hilary turned to her.

"What do you like doing?" she asked.

Bridget, addressed, blinked hurriedly and drew back her head. So it was Mrs. Sanders who answered: "She's a great reader."

"What do you like reading?"

"Take Hilary and show her your books, my dear."

They rose from the table, and Bridget folded her table napkin with great care; then with a quick sidelong glance at Hilary she led the way upstairs.

As soon as they entered Bridget's room, Hilary made straight for the books and began to examine their backs. Many of them she knew.

"I've read that, and that—" she said, and, "Have you

read . . ?" and reeled off a list of some of her favorites; "Ah, yes, you've got that one." Her questions had received no reply, so she turned round. Bridget was sitting on the bed, her hands curling nervously in her lap. "Have you read . . ?" she asked, and she repeated the list more slowly.

Bridget looked up, surprised to find that an answer was required of her. She seemed in doubt what to say, and then muttered, "Er—no."

Hilary began to tell her what the books were about, recommending the ones that she liked best, meanwhile running her eye over the books on the shelf and interrupting herself to ask, "What is this about?" Bridget sat silently on the bed, until Hilary asked a question to which she seemed to require an answer.

"Is it exciting? This book, I mean. Do you like it?"

Bridget opened her mouth, looking rather as if she had been dazzled by headlights. Then she saw a way out. "Borrow it, if you like," she said.

"May I?" asked Hilary, eagerly.

"Yes, if you want to."

"I say, that's awfully nice of you." Hilary brought the book and sat down next to her on the bed. "It looks awfully exciting. I wonder what happens. No, don't tell me"—not that there was any danger of that—"It would spoil the story." Then she shut the book firmly and said, "I really ought to go. My mother will be wondering where I am."

When they got downstairs Mrs. Sanders came out of the kitchen. Hilary thanked her for the tea and said: "Bridget must come to tea with us."

This was what Mrs. Sanders was hoping for, and without reference to Bridget, who bit her lip in the background, they arranged for her to go to tea with the Tofts on the Friday.

"And then you can see *my* books and borrow one," said Hilary.

TWO

A Garden All to Oneself

The next day and on the Friday, which was the day after, Hilary was very pleased with herself and her achievement in having made the acquaintance of the new girl. The other girls were still interested in Bridget with her strange manner. At recess they were discussing her and Hilary took the opportunity to announce, "She's coming to tea with me, you know."

"Is she?" There was envy in the tone in which this was asked and Hilary felt very important. Although she was supposed to be so tactless, she was the only girl with whom Bridget was coming to tea.

"Don't be so pleased with yourself," said someone. They found Hilary's complacent smile annoying. "You'd better not talk too much. She'll find it boring. Let her get a word in sometimes."

Catherine smiled at this, but she did not join in the teasing.

"She never says anything anyway," retorted Hilary.

"Well, that's better than some people who never stop."

But none of their jibes could upset Hilary, who just flicked her plaits over her shoulders and said, "Well, she's not coming to tea with you, anyway," and grinned more broadly.

After school on Friday she and Bridget set off down Holland Park Avenue together. They made an ill-matched pair—Bridget thin and pasty, shorthaired and unnaturally tidy, and Hilary who was on the plump side and ruddy, and untidy with her long dark hair coming in wisps out of her pigtails. When they had walked a little way, Bridget suddenly stopped and, summoning up all her courage, said: "I'd much rather not come."

Hilary was taken aback; this, after all her boasting.

"But what will your aunt say? My mother is expecting you. She'll have made a cake. Your aunt won't have any tea for you. What'll you say to her?"

"I needn't go home. I can just walk around."

"But you can't do that!" Hilary exclaimed. "And have no tea. And in January, too. You'd have to walk jolly hard to keep yourself warm. Just think of all the shoe leather you'd wear out. Oh, come on, you can't!"

Bridget said nothing to this, so she changed her tone. "And what can I say to my mother? She'll have made a cake and all, and she just won't believe it if I say you wouldn't come when it was all arranged. Besides, I thought you wanted to see my books."

Bridget had screwed up all her courage to say she didn't want to come and she had none left to meet Hilary's objections. She just looked at the pavement and reddened a bit, and then they walked on. She had given in, and was miserable about it. Hilary tried to comfort her.

"You must meet my mother, you know," she said. "You'll like her—everyone likes her. She's kind and quiet and not a bit like me. I don't take after her at all. I suppose I take after my father, who is rather a talker. But don't worry; he won't be there. He's never in to tea. There'll just be me and mummy. And my brother David of course. But he's older than me and won't take any notice of us, as he thinks himself far too superior. He'll just eat his tea in a grand, aloof manner and you needn't take any notice of him either. He's not worth it. And after tea he'll just slope off and we won't see him again. So it's really just mummy and me, and mummy will have made a cake and afterwards you can look at my books."

Thus Hilary laid out the program for the evening in the way she thought would be most attractive to her new friend. "You didn't really want not to come, did you?" she asked.

As usual Bridget was startled at being required to speak. After a pause she said, "Ah," rather inaudibly. It could have been taken either way, as a Yes or a No. Hilary took it as a Yes.

All this time they had been climbing the steep slope of Ladbroke Grove and at this moment they reached the top where the road dives down again into the depths of Notting Dale. Hilary, who had been talking all the way up the hill, paused for breath, and they stood for a moment together, looking down the way they had come to the treetops of Holland Park which showed on the hill opposite. The sight of the trees started Hilary on the track of another idea.

"I wish we had a garden," she said, when she had got back enough breath to speak. "I mean, we've got a garden, I know, but it's only the size of a pocket handkerchief, though it's bigger than yours,"—for the houses in Banbury Terrace had little more than back yards with a pretence of earth that was really mostly brickbats. "And I suppose even that is quite good for London. But what I mean is a really big garden. I wish we lived in one of the houses round here which share a common garden with their neighbors. In that way they get really quite big gardens, sort of private parks, with all sorts of different trees and little hidden alleyways, and only the people who live in the houses can go into them."

Then a most surprising thing happened. Bridget began to speak.

"But, still, there would be lots of people using a common garden like that . . ." Then she paused and Hilary said, "Yes?"

"I was just thinking of that garden you were talking about the other day that was quite empty during the War."

"Kew Gardens?"

"Yes. I should like a garden all private like that, one all to myself that no one else knew about."

Hilary was surprised that her random conversation had fallen on such attentive ears, and the surprise made her think for a moment. They walked on in an unexpected silence.

"A few years ago," Hilary said, as they started down Hereford Villas, "some of these common gardens were as deserted as Kew in the War. The houses were bombed and no one lived there, and the gardens were left to grow wild. Nobody went into them, and the grass grew long—waist high—and weeds everywhere. They weren't like ordinary town gardens any longer, more exciting, more sort of private, if you know what I mean. But now the people are back, the lawns are mown and there's always someone walking about with a pram or something. Anyway, here's our house."

At either side of the foot of the steps which led up to the front door of the house stood a pedestal; one of these pedestals was most impressively occupied by an enormous black cat, who had assumed the pose of one of Landseer's lions in Trafalgar Square.

"This is Pip," said Hilary, tickling him behind the ear. Pip received their caresses with a most superior and nonchalant air and, when they went up the steps, rose with great dignity and followed them.

The tea party was not the trial and agony that Bridget had anticipated. As Hilary had prophesied, she took immediately to Mrs. Toft, who had a way of making her feel quite comfortable even while she preserved her habitual silence. Somehow Bridget felt part of the conversation even without having to contribute to it. So often people seemed to talk at her, daring her to speak; but here she felt no necessity to open her mouth and yet she was within the circle, not excluded from it.

This first tea party broke the ice to such an extent that others followed without much effort, and Bridget became a familiar figure at the house in Hereford Villas. The traffic of books that had started on the first day of acquaintance continued during the weeks that followed. Every time that Bridget came to Hilary's, she took a different book back with her, and Hilary often walked home by way of Bridget's house and called in to change a book. At first she chose for herself from the shelves, but one day Bridget rather haltingly took down a book and pushed it across to her saying: "This . . . er . . . I like this one very much. I don't know if you would."

Hilary took it, asking, "What is it about?"

Bridget answered: "It's about a garden, just like the ones you were talking about, that were empty after the bombing. See, the book's called *The Secret Garden.*"

Hilary remembered particularly clearly how Bridget had shown a sudden interest in gardens, because it was the only time she had ever launched independently into speech. Because it was connected with this occasion, Hilary could not help feeling excited when she settled down to read the book. Bridget was still very much of a mystery to her and she felt that the book might have the answers to some of her questions. There had been a good deal of speculation in the class about Bridget's past history, as everyone agreed that it was decidedly odd for anyone to be as shy and silent as she was. No one had succeeded in getting her to utter more than one or two words. She had not proved to be very good at lessons, with one notable exception: she could read and write French without any difficulty, and would even sometimes speak it in class, with an accent which everybody agreed sounded more French than the French mistress's. "Perhaps she's partly French," someone suggested. But when asked, Bridget replied with a hasty, yet decisive, no.

"Now," thought Hilary, "I shall find out everything. In this book are the clues, and I shall follow them until I get to the bottom of the mystery." She threw herself down on the hearthrug and was soon absorbed. A silence fell on the house that was unusual when Hilary was at home, and just as, when a clock stops, one becomes aware of the cessation of the ticking, so the Toft family noticed the unaccustomed silence.

"What's Hilary doing?" asked David. "It's so quiet."

"Hush," said his mother. "Let sleeping dogs lie. She is only reading some book Bridget loaned her."

"That all? I'd not have thought it."

Meanwhile Hilary was too absorbed to notice. The book fascinated her. "Why ever did I think I wanted to go about in boats?" she wondered. "Nothing could be a patch on having a garden like the one the little girl in the story found. I wonder if we could do the same, somehow. There might still be places. There were, a few years ago." She thought of the deserted gardens she had known just after the War, which she had spoken of to Bridget. There were several that she had passed daily on her way to school. She had known them first as ordinary town gardens before the houses were bombed. Then after the bombing, when she went in the morning to school, the ruins were still smoking and there were firemen working amongst the rubble. Later, static water tanks had been built where the bombs had fallen, and the neighboring houses which were still standing, though without windows or roofs, were reflected in their dismal depths. After the War the cement cracked and the tanks stood empty; seeds of willow herb lodged in the cracks, and in late summer a riot of pink flowers rose to hide the tin cans and refuse that people had thrown there. Meanwhile the gardens behind had been left to themselves. Nobody lived there, so nobody bothered to look after them, and they had run wild.

Hilary could remember one spring, soon after the end of the War, when these deserted gardens had been carpeted in bluebells. Perhaps they had been like that every year—but this one spring she had come alive to this rippling carpet of blue, which had spread itself where only ghosts could walk. Between the palings of the fences which enclosed these gardens she had gazed at this wild, secret woodland, derelict and lonely in the midst of buzzing London—and in imagination she entered and wandered there, and made the place her own. But soon after that spring the houses had begun to be repaired and rebuilt, and the people had come back, and now the gardens were ordered and frequented.

"Well," she said to herself, "those places are no good any longer. The people are back. They're just ordinary London gardens once more, with people with prams and suchlike, and lawn mowers going all the time. But there may still be others . . ."

She thought of all the bombed sites she knew. There were still plenty in that part of London. Perhaps one that she had never bothered to explore might have a garden still deserted even now, which she and Bridget could make their own secret garden. It was well worth looking, she thought.

◆ THREE ◆

The Search Begins

During the next fortnight Hilary made a systematic search for a garden. As she had said, she knew that part of London fairly well. She knew where the possibilities lay. After school each day, when she had left Bridget where their ways parted, she would set off for some objective she had planned to explore. But day after day her search proved unsuccessful. Bombed sites remained in plenty, but there were none which even her active imagination could transform into a secret garden. All such real gardens as there were had been reclaimed by their rightful owners since the War.

All this time her friendship with Bridget continued, and they often went about together. But an unexpected change had come over Hilary. She no longer held forth, covering Bridget's silence with the flood of her eloquence. All the time they were together Hilary's mind was filled with the possibility of the garden, which, if found, she felt sure would have a magical effect upon Bridget, as the secret garden had had upon the children in the story. And because her thoughts were elsewhere she found it difficult to keep up a flow of casual conversation. She felt awkward. She was determined not to talk of the garden until it was found, and there seemed to be nothing else to talk about.

To everyone's surprise Hilary seemed to be much more subdued than usual. When she was with Bridget, she spent her time puzzling about her and wondering whether she was unhappy; and again and again she told herself, "I must find that garden, I really must!"

At the end of the fortnight Hilary felt that she had exhausted all the possibilities, and almost gave up hope. But on the Tuesday of the next week, she had remembered another place. It was her last hope, and when she parted with Bridget after school, she said she "had something to do."

When she had crossed Holland Park Avenue, Hilary went up one side of Campden Hill Square. It was a steep climb, for Holland Park Avenue runs along a narrow valley with hills on either side. Soon after she had turned the corner at the top, the huge and gloomy water tower loomed up in front of her. It was a place that had always, strangely, filled her with horror and now it made her stop and say, "This place isn't going to be any good. Why go on?" A gust of wind came down the street and blustered eerily up the side of the grim, grey tower.

"But, no," Hilary said, pulling herself together, "I want to *know* that this place is no good. Otherwise, I won't be satisfied."

The place that she was making for was a bombed site where, the year before, she had gone on Guy Fawkes night with some friends, to let off a few fireworks—the first she had ever seen, since there had been none during the War. She had seen the site only in the dark; so, she thought, it may be just the place I'm looking for. But when she arrived there, it was just like many other bombed sites. From the pavement she could see the whole place. A block of houses had gone, and their basements stood open to the sky. Behind, their back gardens had merged into one.

"It's too public," she said aloud. "And yet . . ."

It was better than many places she had seen; more overgrown than most. Even in February, with the greenery gone, it looked wild and entangled. Briars and brambles trailed down into the basements and made them look more like natural chasms and caves. Even the electric wiring, sagging away from the wall, did not dispel the illusion, and in one kitchen a sycamore sapling had broken through the tiled floor.

Despite its being so public, Hilary was tempted to explore. She made her way round to where it was easy to get onto the site and then started to wander along where little paths had formed amongst the undergrowth and rubble. A moment before she had thought the place empty. Now she saw a movement and—before she had time to notice where they came from—a gang of large boys had suddenly sprung up round her. At first she thought they were all huge. Then, when she had had time to look, she saw that they ranged in age from a little, and extremely

dirty, boy of about six, who stood in the front, to a large uncouth-looking youth in his teens, who now made himself the spokesman.

"Look who's here!" he said in a jeering voice.

"I might say the same of you," replied Hilary.

"And what might you be doing here?"

"That's none of your business."

"That's none of your business," he mimicked. His minions began to snigger derisively.

"As a matter of fact I'm just passing through," said

Hilary. She felt her face getting hot. The brutes! "Do you mind getting out of my way?" They were blocking the path.

"Do you mind getting out of my way?" he mimicked again, and when his gang had sniggered once more, he said, "Oh, no! It's a pleasure, my dear," and with a mock bow he made a passage through the middle of them.

Her ears burning, Hilary marched through. As she walked away she could feel their eyes on her back. The smallest boy, the six-year-old, shouted abuse after her, using the foulest language. "Don't take any notice of them," she said to herself. Unfortunately she stumbled on some rubble, and the blood rushed to her face with embarrassment.

"Upsy daisy!" she heard one of them shout behind her, followed by guffaws.

"A most unsuitable place," she said to herself as she hurried home to tea.

FOUR

A Day at Kew

So there was to be no secret garden. Hilary made up her mind to it and swallowed her disappointment. "It has been a stupid dream really," she said to herself, "though a very pleasant one. And, of course, it would have made no difference to Bridget." But in her heart of hearts she continued to believe that the garden was the one thing that would bring Bridget out of her shell. "Out of her shell," thought Hilary; "yes, that is a very good expression. There are times when she looks just like a snail drawing in its horns and drawing itself back into its shell."

This thought passed through Hilary's mind one day when Bridget had come to tea and Mrs. Toft began to unfold a plan of hers.

"I've been thinking," she said. "It's your half term next weekend. If the weather continues that we've had these last two days, we might go out for a jaunt on the Monday. Kew would not be crowded on a Monday so early in the year, even a sunny one, I think. It might even be warm enough to take a picnic lunch—one never knows at this time of year. There would be just the three of us. That is, if you would like to come, Bridget?"

"There," thought Hilary, "she looks just like a snail drawing itself hastily into its shell." Aloud she said, "Oh do come! We could have such a lovely time."

"I don't know what my aunt would say," said Bridget for an excuse. One might almost have thought she was being trapped into a most unpleasant engagement from the way she tried to slip out of it. Really she would have loved to go, but she was afraid to commit herself, or tie herself up, by agreeing outright.

Hilary would have burst in at this point, protesting that Mrs. Sanders was sure to let Bridget come and that she must come or she would spoil all the fun, and so on. In this way she would probably have frightened Bridget out of coming altogether; but luckily Mrs. Toft got in first. Very gently she removed Bridget's excuse from under her feet by telling her that she had already spoken to Mrs. Sanders. She added that, of course, if Bridget did not think she would enjoy it, they did not want to force her into it. She told her the things they would probably do, and made them sound very attractive, somehow or other suppressing her daughter, who was all the while eager to speak. And when she had finished she said, "Now, don't you burst in, Hilary," so that Bridget had time to say, "I should like to come very much, thank you, Mrs. Toft."

Thus it was settled, and the changeful English weather was kind for once and fell in with their arrangements.

On the day they had fixed there was a good wind blowing and chasing the clouds across the sky like new-washed linen that had come off the line. "It's a perfect washing day," said Mrs. Toft, sniffing the air, "and I think a perfect day for our purposes too. In fact, I shall pack some sandwiches. Out of the wind it will probably be warm enough to eat outside."

Mr. Toft and David had both had their breakfast and gone, but Bridget had not yet arrived, and Hilary was jumping up and down in nervous agitation.

"I do believe she doesn't mean to come after all! What's the time? Shall I see if she's coming down the street?"

"My dear," said her mother reprovingly, "it's only a quarter past eight. I think we might allow her a little more time before giving her up for lost. Couldn't you help me butter this bread instead of running out into the street, which won't bring her here any faster anyway?"

Hilary came into the kitchen and began to spread margarine on the bread her mother had cut.

"You must put it on thinner than that, my dear. Remember, it's rationed."

Hilary made up for the thickness of the margarine by slicing the cucumber so thin that it was quite transparent and almost invisible.

"Isn't she a funny girl, Mummy?" she said, puzzling as she worked. "What do you think made her like that?"

"Like what, dear?"

"So shy. Like a rabbit that bolts at the very sight of

you. Like a snail that draws into its shell, when you speak to her. Do you think it's being an orphan that makes her like that?"

"I think it has a great deal to do with it."

"But why should it, Mummy? I mean, why should it have that effect? I mean, if you and Daddy had both been killed in the War—I'm jolly glad you weren't, of course, but if you had been—I don't think I should have stopped talking and shut up inside myself like that."

Mrs. Toft laughed. "No, I don't think you would."

"Then why should she have, Mummy?"

"People aren't all the same, dear; you must have noticed that. They aren't all as bouncing and resilient as you. I daresay Bridget was always a shy, silent girl. Her parents must have meant a great deal to her, being an only child. When she lost them, she had no one to turn to, and so she became shyer and more silent than ever. I hope that one of these days she will find someone she can turn to, just as she turned to her own mother, and then she will open out again."

"Hmm," said Hilary, not satisfied, but thinking it over.

Mrs. Toft was wondering if she should tell Hilary the things she had learnt about Bridget's history from Mrs. Sanders. For as soon as she had met Bridget she had decided that she must get to know Mrs. Sanders and by now she knew a good deal more than Hilary did about her friend. But, knowing how tactless her daughter was, she decided not to speak.

"But do you think she's happy?" asked Hilary. "She never smiles. Can she be very happy if she never talks to anyone and has no friends?"

"People are happy in different ways, Hilary. They don't all have to talk the whole time. But, no, I don't think Bridget is happy."

"I wonder if her aunt is very kind to her. She didn't seem to me to be a very understanding sort of woman, like you, Mummy. Now, if she lived with you, I am sure Bridget would soon open out."

Just then the bell rang and Hilary dropped the cucumber on the floor in her haste to answer it. But her mother barred her way.

"I'm sure Mrs. Sanders does her very best for Bridget. You must not picture her as a wicked stepmother. It would be most unfair." And then she let her go.

Bridget stood on the doorstep, a little flushed with haste.

"We'd almost given you up for lost," cried Hilary. "I thought you'd turned tail at the idea of spending a whole day in my company. But you do want to come, don't you?"

"Oh yes," said Bridget, surprised as usual, but pleased all the same.

"You've come just at the right time," said Mrs. Toft. "We have only this minute finished making the sandwiches. Can you help me? You will be much more use than Hilary at packing them up. Here is some greaseproof paper. These are cucumber. Hilary has sliced it so thin that I don't think we shall taste it at all. But she spent so much time talking that she didn't have a hand in anything else."

"Mummy did the tomato ones and put such whopping lumps of tomato in, that the sandwiches won't close up."

Soon they were ready and going for the bus.

"We'll take a 27. It goes all the way," said Mrs. Toft. "Slower than the Underground, I think, but you see all London en route."

"If we get a place at the front on top," added Hilary.

They did.

"It hardly feels as if half a term had gone by yet," said Hilary. "Do you feel like that, Bridget? It seems only yesterday when I think of the beginning of term; and yet we're half way through it."

"Bridget has met so many people and it has all been new to her and that, I daresay, has made it seem like an eternity to her," said Mrs. Toft. Bridget caught her eye as Mrs. Toft smiled at her, and as the words echoed so well her own thoughts she burst out with an "Oh, yes." Then, having spoken so eagerly and thus revealed what she thought, she was convulsed with embarrassment.

So Mrs. Toft, to draw their attention away from her embarrassment, cried out, "Look! Did you see that? The most enormous tabby cat curled up in an antique shop window." They were going down Church Street now.

"I wonder if the shopkeeper knows it's there," said Hilary. "Cats are so dainty in their stepping that I am sure it would never knock anything over."

"You forget that Pip smashed four of my best cups and saucers and two plates the Christmas before last."

"Ah, but then Pip is so fond of fruit cake that when

he's once on the track of that he's blind to anything else."

"Does he really eat fruit cake?" asked Bridget in surprise.

"Oh yes, it's one of his favorites."

Mrs. Toft felt that the day promised really well since Bridget had made a remark of her own accord, and she listened, smiling, while Hilary recounted all the strange habits and escapades of Pip.

The bus took them west along Kensington High Street and presently stopped outside a large cinema. Bridget was looking out on the opposite side of the bus, to her right, and Mrs. Toft pointed out to her the remains of Holland House that showed amongst the treetops of Holland Park.

"It was burnt down in the War," she said. "And not far away," she went on, "you can see the treetops of some of the big gardens of the old houses on Campden Hill. I always used to think, before the War, how nice it would be to live up there. Some of the houses were built long before this part was London at all, when it was still in the country, and they still have really big country gardens. But I believe many of them were bombed in the War and are still standing derelict. In time, I daresay, they'll be pulled down and big blocks of apartment houses built instead. Land in London is too valuable to be wasted on private gardens."

If only Hilary had been attending at that moment instead of reading out the film advertisements and declaring that she wondered what the film was all about! By the time the bus moved on, she had missed all that her mother had said.

So the bus went on, and all through Hammersmith and Chiswick, Hilary talked about this and that and never a thought entered her head of the secret garden, which she had now given up as impossible. But Bridget all the time was lost in a dream of those deserted gardens of the bombed houses on Campden Hill. Hilary had certainly had more insight than was usually hers when she had thought that the secret garden was very close to Bridget's heart.

Once in Kew, Hilary was reminded of the secret garden. When she and Bridget had first met, it was the subject of Kew that had roused Bridget's interest and made her speak of her desire for a garden. "I'll tell her I have looked for a garden," thought Hilary. "She will be interested, even if there isn't one to be found. But not now," she added to herself; "it must be in secret."

As it was chilly they did not linger long except in the hot houses. After lunch they decided to warm themselves up with a brisk walk along the towpath to Richmond.

"I think it will rain after all," said Hilary, looking up at the sky.

There was indeed little doubt that it would rain. The clouds had massed up in thick blackening banks and the glimpses of sunlight had gone. The wind that had seemed gay and turbulent before had suddenly become sinister and purposeful. It blew upon the black surface of the river, sending restless fretful waves in gusts towards the shore.

"It looks like a storm. We must hurry, and even then we shall be soaked," said Mrs. Toft.

The rain fell suddenly, in large drops.

Mrs. Toft drew instinctively under a tree, although there were no leaves on it and it could afford them little shelter.

"That one would be better," cried Hilary running on, though there was little to choose between the trees. Bridget stood undecided as to whether to follow Hilary or stay with Mrs. Toft. At that moment a woman walking with her dog took shelter under Mrs. Toft's tree and began to comment on the weather. Bridget's horror of strangers decided her. She ran on.

"Stand against the trunk like this," said Hilary, "then you get the most shelter. . . . Why, it's hail!" she added as the heavy patter of rain was replaced by the clipped clatter of hailstones on the hard path. She leaned out to catch them, but they melted in her hot hands as she turned to show her catch to Bridget.

As her eyes met those of Bridget, who seemed to be excited and roused by the storm, she remembered that she was going to tell her about her search for the garden. Grey curtains of driving hail had isolated them from the rest of the world, and left them in secret. It was the very moment for the telling of confidences.

"You know, Bridget," she said, lowering her voice, "I had been thinking, ever since you loaned me that book, that one might be able to find a secret garden here in London."

Bridget made an incoherent sound, perhaps of surprise, but anyway of interest.

"I've looked everywhere. There were lots of places I thought of, and I have explored them all, I think. I don't know, but I think I've looked in all the possible places and none of them is possible. You know what I mean? They could none of them be secret, really. All the best places are occupied again now, and kept in order."

"Do you think," said Bridget suddenly, "there are some places you haven't thought of?" She was going to ask about the houses on Campden Hill. Perhaps, anyway, Hilary had explored them and they were no good.

"Well, I mean, there might be, perhaps. But I can't think of any. Of course there are a lot of bombed sites in our part of London. They're exciting in a way, with the cellars open and overgrown, with kitchen sinks all amongst bushes so that indoors and outdoors are all mixed up. But none of them are very private, or could be secret, you know. People walk there with their dogs and take short cuts through them. Everyone goes there. Sometimes, even, horrid gangs of boys have taken them over."

All during this speech Bridget had been preparing herself to ask about the houses on Campden Hill, but now that a pause occurred she could not think how to say it. She started to stutter something like "I just—I just wondered," when the happy thought occurred to her that another day would do just as well to ask her question. Indeed, that moment suddenly seemed to her to be most unsuitable. The hail was abating. Might not Mrs. Toft appear at any moment?

"I just tell you all this," said Hilary, "about the bombed sites and so on, to show you the sort of possibilities I had in mind. But now I don't really think it's possible. We might find something of course. We just might. It would be so nice," she added wistfully.

"Yes," said Bridget, concurring. Another day she would mention Campden Hill. Perhaps Hilary had not thought of it.

Just then Mrs. Toft came up, for the hail had changed to rain and was falling only in a very desultory manner.

"We must hurry, before it starts up again. Come on, you two, we must get home."

FIVE

The Very Place

But Bridget never asked her question. Day by day she put if off, and day by day it became more difficult to ask, until she became almost frightened of asking it. Perhaps Hilary was no longer interested in a garden, she thought. Then she would look a fool, bringing it up again. Or perhaps Hilary had already thought of her place—the gardens Mrs. Toft had pointed out from the top of the bus. Then, again, she would look a fool. Hilary would say, "Of course, I looked there," perhaps rather snubbingly.

Bridget thought she might look for the place herself, but she did not know how to find her way, so she gave up that idea. But she could not get rid of the idea of the gardens on Campden Hill. And The Question, which she would ask Hilary tomorrow, perhaps, if she dared, assumed enormous proportions in her mind. When with Hilary she could think of nothing else, and because she never asked it she became more withdrawn and shyer than ever.

Other things contributed to her increasing shyness. At home, life was far from happy. Mrs. Sanders had intended to be kind to the little orphan, but however hard she tried she could not feel very affectionate toward so silent and unfriendly a child. Although she felt sorry for Bridget and would have liked to have seen her happy, she could not help becoming more and more irritated by Bridget's silent behavior. Mrs. Sanders was cross with herself for being cross with Bridget, but that did not help. It only made her feel more impatient and bad tempered than usual. Sometimes she lost her temper. Then Bridget withdrew further into her shell and Mrs. Sanders felt more irritated than ever. And so it went on.

At school, too, the girls, who had at first been kind, became bored with her and some got into the habit of bullying and teasing her.

Hilary noticed that Bridget had become shyer. "Just when we were getting on so well," she thought. It puzzled her. She could not guess why, instead of becoming friendlier after they had talked about the garden, Bridget was back where she had been at the very beginning. Again and again Hilary attempted to be friendly once more, but Bridget seemed to avoid her. "I can't make her out at all," said Hilary to herself. "I give it up. I thought she would like to be friends with me, but now I believe she doesn't want to."

By now Hilary had read most of Bridget's books and Bridget no longer seemed to want to borrow hers. Mrs. Toft began to notice that Bridget no longer came to the house. She was sorry, because she had begun to take a real interest in her. One day she suggested that Hilary should ask her to tea.

"Yes, I will," said Hilary, "but she hasn't wanted to come recently."

The next day she forgot about her invitation until the end of the afternoon, and then, when she went to look for Bridget in the cloakroom, she found she had already slipped off. While she was wondering what to do she saw Catherine, Bridget's appointed guardian, leaving the cloak-room.

"She may be able to tell me if there's anything wrong," she thought, and flung on her shoes and coat and rushed after her.

Now Catherine was a quiet and sensible girl with a great sense of responsibility. But she was also unassuming, so that she was quite popular, which some girls who have the reputation for being good—and let everyone know it—are not. Being quiet herself she had accepted Bridget's quietness from the first and had spoken little to her. She was always ready to help her and show her what to do, but she did not try to pry open the shell of her shyness. Bridget was often to be found at her side. It was a safe place for her to be, where she was accepted and helped without the necessity of saying anything and where no one would tease her.

"What's come over Bridget lately?" asked Hilary, as she caught up with Catherine.

"What d'you mean?"

"She's become as shy as she was at the beginning and just when she'd begun to talk and smile a little more."

"I haven't noticed it."

"Well, I have. She used to come round to my house, of her own accord without my persuading her, before half term, but she doesn't now. And when I talk to her she's only keen to get away."

"Well, can you blame her?" asked Catherine.

"Don't be provoking. Why don't you answer my question?"

"Honestly, Hilary, I haven't noticed this change you speak of. She's always been shy."

Hilary changed her tack. "I want to help Bridget, and I think she's unhappy. You were put in charge of her. Don't you want to help her?"

"I don't think you are helping her, Hilary. She doesn't want to be talked to all the time."

"How do you know? You haven't asked her. You think you know all there is to know about her just because you were put in charge of her. Well, you don't. I know more than you do. You may think I'm just a nuisance interfering in your domain but Bridget liked me all right. I daresay it's you that's set her up against me."

"I'm sorry," Catherine said. "But look here, Hilary, I haven't set Bridget against you. And I don't mean to be nasty, Hilary, but you *are* tactless. You must admit it. You never know when people have had enough of you. Bridget's shy, and if she doesn't want you always hanging on to her tail you'd be doing your best to help her if you left her alone."

And with this she turned to cross the road and go up Holland Walk, which was her way home.

Now Hilary was certainly a tactless girl and she never saw a hint with however loud a crash it dropped to the ground. Otherwise when she had heard Catherine say, "You never know when people have had enough of you" she would have refrained from forcing her company on her any longer. As it was she crossed the road and turned up Holland Walk with her, although her way lay in the opposite direction. But she wanted to go on arguing her point. Into the bottom of her heart had entered a fear that perhaps Catherine was right, which could only be removed by convincing Catherine of the opposite.

"Aren't you going home?" asked her victim. But it needed more than that to get rid of Hilary.

"I'll just walk a little way with you," she said and they started the steep climb where Holland Walk leaves the valley of the road and scales Campden Hill. "You see," Hilary went on, "it's not only me—and I know I'm tactless—but it's my mother, too. Bridget used to come and talk to her, but she doesn't any longer. Everyone knows that my mother isn't tactless like me but that she's just the opposite, and the very mother Bridget wants as she's lost her own. Besides which, we have a lot of things in common, Bridget and I."

"Oh, indeed," said Catherine, amused. "And what might they be?"

"Oh well, hmm, reading. And there are other things too," said Hilary vaguely, for no one should know their secret.

To hide her confusion at so nearly having given herself away, Hilary looked at her surroundings. Suddenly she realized that this was the first time she had been up Holland Walk.

"Why," she said, "I've never been along here before."

"And I don't know why you're coming along here now."

"It's nice to explore. Interesting, I mean. What's behind this fence?"

It was a high slatted fence and Hilary ran her knuckles along it, making a thunderous rattle as they jumped from slat to slat.

"You will get a splinter in your hand," said Catherine dispassionately, as if it did not matter in the least to her. "Holland Park is behind there."

One could not look over the fence, as it was too high, nor was it the sort one could look through.

"Can one go inside?"

"No, it's shut up. They might open it to the public one day, or so they say, but it's shut up now."

"Can one get in anywhere, I mean, just sneak in? Would you know?"

"No, you can't get in anywhere. Nowhere at all."

So that was that.

"What's over there?" asked Hilary pointing with her thumb across the lane, which was bounded on the other side by a high brick garden wall.

"Gardens, I suppose. I don't know. The houses have been bombed and no one lives there."

"Oh," said Hilary, doing her best to hide her elation.

There was a door in the wall, and on it was written in uneven lettering of chalk:

Whoever enters here never comes out again.

To Hilary such a mysterious warning was as good as an invitation. It seemed to suggest that one could, if one dared, enter quite easily. Immediately she felt quite sure that here was the garden she had been looking for. Out loud she said, "I think I'd better be getting back now."

"I've been thinking that for some time," said Catherine. "Good-bye." And she walked on.

Hilary turned and walked back until she reached a place where a slight turning in the lane hid her from the other girl, and there she stood against the wall, waiting and counting her heartbeats. Her heart was pounding hard in her excitement.

A minute or two elapsed. Holland Walk was silent and empty. There was nothing but the patter of twigs blown against the slatted palings. Hilary started to walk cautiously back up under the fence. Catherine had gone. She was alone. She was opposite the door with its ominous inscription now, and, looking in both directions, she saw that there was no one in sight. She crossed the alleyway and put her shoulder to the door and her hand to the latch. The click of the latch resounded in the silence so that she thought the whole world must hear, but the door did not move. It must be locked or bolted.

So with an exaggerated carelessness Hilary stepped out of the doorway into the lane. There was still no one there to see her. She stood undecided as to which way to turn. Surely she was not to be disappointed when her hopes had come so near to realization. There must be some way into the garden behind the wall. She walked along slowly, examining the wall for possible footholds.

Presently a man came walking down the lane, so Hilary walked quickly on, pretending to be interested in the fence on the other side. When the intruder's footsteps had ceased to sound upon the pavement she turned round to see if he was really gone.

Yes, he was gone. But Hilary hardly noticed the fact. She stood, her eyes nearly popping out of her head, staring at the wall opposite. For at this point all the upper part of it had been knocked down, either by a bomb or by a falling tree, and where the gash was lowest it only stood as high as her shoulders.

Hilary was an agile girl, though on the plump side.

She measured the wall up against herself and then felt along the top for a good place to put her hands. She took a little run and jump and then hoisted her legs up after herself.

All the debris and masonry from the wall had fallen on the inside and was piled up against it, so that there was no drop down. Some barbed wire was slung across the gap but that was easy enough to get under. She was inside. Inside the Secret Garden. She stepped forward slowly, wonderingly, a little gingerly. It was incredible. Had she really ever thought she would find such a place? Yet here she was, inside.

The garden was very dark, or perhaps that was the day. The sky was heavy and leaden overhead and under her feet the ivy had run amuck and swathed path and tree and bush in its black pall. The black rank smell of it caught her nostrils as she crushed it under her feet. She walked in what had once been a shrubbery, down what had once been a path; one could see where the bushes stood apart, though the ivy sprawled everywhere without distinction.

Hilary walked slowly, treading carefully amongst the ivy and peering to the right and left amongst the bushes that were embedded in its growth. The garden was very still and strange. Footsteps went past down Holland Walk but they seemed so remote that they might have come from another world. The garden was apart, a world to itself.

Presently she saw the door in the wall. Here on the inside it was curtained with ivy. "That's just as it should be," she thought. "Just like the door that led into the secret garden in Bridget's book." She went to examine it, lifting the ivy to see the bolts. There they were, rusted fast in their places. No wonder she had not been able to open the door.

She wandered on, breathing in the stillness of the neglected place. "No one has trodden here for so long," she thought. There stood a great earth-filled urn, in a circle of seats. They had been painted once, but what color it would be hard to say, as even the flaking remains of paint had mostly disappeared and what was still there had assumed the color of London grime. The ivy had crept up through the slats and fell luxuriantly over the seat. Hilary paused with her hand on the edge of the stone urn and looked into the garden which opened out from here. The shrubbery with its sprawl of ivy was behind her and before her stretched a different sort of wilderness, barer and more open.

"I won't look any further," she said. "Bridget shall come and we can look together."

And she returned by the way she had come.

ও SIX ৪

Bridget Takes the Lead

Hilary told her mother to expect Bridget to tea the next day, and also added, "We'll probably come in late, as we've something to do after school."

This time she did not leave her invitation or her news till the end of the afternoon. In fact she went especially early so as to catch Bridget before prayers. But Bridget herself was late. At recess she caught her, drove her into a dark deserted corner and, in a husky conspiratorial whisper, announced, "I've found it."

"What?" asked Bridget.

"The Garden—the Secret Garden. It's the very place. I'll not tell you about it, because we can go there and explore it. My mother expects you home to tea today, and we can go there on the way back from school. You'll come?"

Bridget's eyes had lit up. "Oh, yes," she exclaimed without hesitation, although there were a hundred excuses she could have offered. She forgot that she ought to tell her aunt and that there was rather a lot of homework to do that night.

They did not speak of the garden again until the end of the day, and each nursed her excitement in anticipation. At the end of the afternoon all the girls packed their books and left the classroom one after another. Bridget was usually one of the first to be ready and gone because she was precise and neat and had everything in order. Also, she was usually eager to escape. Today she lingered, rearranging her books and putting one in and out of her satchel and casting a furtive glance at Hilary, who was as usual the last to be ready. This was not surprising, seeing the state in which she kept her desk; it would never shut and if one looked inside one might think a whirlwind had lately been through it. Long after the others were gone Hilary was still rootling about and sending books out backwards like a dog hunting for a bone.

"I simply can't find my Latin book," she declared and began to throw the books out on the floor in a last attempt, asserting all the time that she had looked *everywhere.*

"Is that it?" asked Bridget picking it out from amongst the books.

"Oh, yes. Good! My desk needs tidying. Well, it's a good thing that the others have all gone, as we don't want them to see where we go. Catherine's gone, I suppose? You see, it's on her way home."

As they walked along Holland Park Avenue, Hilary kept bursting out:

"It's a wonderful place. . . . But I won't tell you. You'll see."

They turned up Holland Walk, and Bridget read the name on the corner out loud.

"Holland Walk." Then suddenly the courage entered into her and she dared to ask the question that she had been putting off for so long. "Is it the garden of one of the old houses next to Holland Park?"

"Yes. Holland Park is on the right here. Our garden is on the other side of the lane."

Bridget was glad that she had been able to ask her question after all, even if its usefulness was past.

They were now at the top of the steep rise and presently were walking between the wall and the fence. Hilary could not resist drawing her hand along the latter because of the noise it made.

"Holland Park is behind here," she said. "But we mustn't make so much noise,"—although only she was making any—"or people will notice us too much. Oh dear, someone's coming."

An old man, very bent and walking slowly and talking to himself, was coming along the walk. Hilary quickly changed the subject and started to talk loudly about their homework in order to disarm suspicion. He did not even seem to notice them and continued his muttered monologue without raising his eyes. The two girls walked quite a distance on beyond their objective before Hilary thought it safe to turn round and go back. The old man had disappeared from the scene when they reached the break in the wall.

"This is where we get in," said Hilary. "Shall I go first? This is how one gets up." She scrambled up herself, and then turned to help Bridget. "Can you do it? Look, I'll get down again and help."

Bridget, though of much the same height and not as fat as Hilary, had not nearly so much power in her muscles. She could not scramble up by herself, so Hilary jumped down and, having taken a good look in both directions to see that the coast was still clear, she tried crouching on the ground while Bridget climbed on her back. In this way they were soon both slipping under the barbed wire, down the rubble, and into the garden.

It had rained hard during the day while they had been at school and the earth was damp and smelled fresh and delicious. It was a smell of spring, suggestive of new growth and of little plants pressing up through the soft reawakening earth ready to unfold their new green leaves after a refreshing shower. The rain was finished now and a south wind was washing the sky clean of clouds. In the walled garden it was still, and the warm air was drawing the steam out of the ground, and raindrops quivered on the leaves. As they walked down the rubble into the garden, the sun came out from behind the last clouds and the sunlight was spattered on the ivy and shrubs, and caught in the quivering raindrops which hung like festoons of diamonds on every twig and leaf; they never ceased to move, each a little prism of light flashing out the colors of the rainbow.

The two girls walked slowly, sniffing the fresh smell, their eyes as bright as the raindrops. Hilary was silent, watching her friend and restraining her eagerness to act as guide. Every now and then Hilary uttered an inarticulate noise as if a half-formed word pent up in her throat had flown to her mouth despite herself. But wonder sealed her lips—wonder at the beauty and reality of the garden, and wonder at Bridget's wonder, so clearly written on her face. For Bridget's face, usually so reserved and tightly drawn, was now lit and fused to life with a strange and wonderful expression; her eyes danced, her lips smiled, there was a flush on her white cheeks and there even seemed to be more flesh on the thin face.

They walked in amongst the shrubs, softly and slowly, and picked their way through the ivy where once the path had led. The earth in the great stone urn was damp and fresh to the touch. They stood together with their hands in it, looking out into the garden.

"I haven't gone further than this," said Hilary.

So they moved forward in silence on to the lawn.

It had once been a lawn, that is. Last summer's grass had grown to waist-high hay and then the wind and rain had flattened it to a brownish matting. Through this the new grass was appearing green, and some other plants besides, which could have had no place on the original lawn. The desolate windowless house stood to their left. Some French windows had once opened out on to the lawn, but now they hung awry on a single hinge and some of the innards of the house seemed to have been dragged out through them—an old rat-eaten mattress and broken furniture were half over the threshold. Some bottomless saucepans which had rolled out on to the grass completed the group.

To Hilary the house was fascinating and she looked at it with curiosity. Bridget only gave it a glance and then turned to the garden which extended to their right beyond

the lawn. It was she, strangely, who took the lead and Hilary who followed.

"I wonder how it was laid out originally," Hilary whispered. The spell seemed to have unbound a little and they found they could talk now, though only in whispers. "That must've been the lawn once and perhaps there were flowers round the edge. And then this was the vegetable garden."

"It could've been flowers set out formally. Often with this type of little low hedge you get flowers in between." Even in the garden Bridget was surprised at herself for having said so much spontaneously and shut her mouth suddenly.

"I should have thought these hedges would have grown higher with being left. They are very ragged now and dead in parts though, aren't they?"

"Oh, they don't grow any higher. They can't, I think, the dwarf ones. Anyway, these are much higher than they should be, and broader."

These little dwarf box hedges, or what was left of them, marked the edges of former beds and the network of pathways running in between them. The paths, which had been trodden so hard in times past, were less overgrown than the beds, where now the dry bones of last year's dead growth made a hollow blackened forest. Grime coated thickly these depressing remains and it came off on Hilary's hand as she fingered the stalks.

"They *are* dirty," she said, wiping her hand on her mack. "But what can you expect in London? What are these? Look how they're curled; it makes them look quite decorative, doesn't it?"

"That's willow herb. It has long thin seed pods, and then they split open to let the seeds out and the sides of the pod curl back like that. See, all this group of curls would have made one pod."

"What, willow herb? The same with the pink flowers that grows all over London bombed sites? Well, well, and I never knew it looked like this afterwards. I like it. It has a kind of swirling energy to look at. But it's so dirty." She had handled it again, and so had Bridget in pointing out the structure. Bridget took out her handkerchief and wiped her hands carefully on it, unlike Hilary who wiped hers on her mack again.

They threaded their way slowly amongst the beds, talking in lowered voices.

"What are these that look like candelabras? I've never

seen one as big as this before. Why, it must be about ten feet high!"

"They are hemlock, I think."

There was a forest of them, towering above the other dried sticks of plants like forest trees over bushes and shrubs. Some of the great heads were at least two feet across and they seemed as tall as the apple trees nearby.

"It is a long time since those were pruned," said Bridget. One could see the shape to which they had once been pruned, but above that point the new growth had shot up vertically to about twice the height the trees had once been.

"You know much more about plants and gardens than I do," said Hilary; "but those I recognize. They are dead nettles—stinging nettles that are dead, I mean—not dead nettles. And a whole new crop's coming up underneath. It will be a sea of nettles soon."

"They are nice to eat cooked, when they are young like that."

"Have you ever tried them?"

"Yes, we ate them during the War, and the old ones too, but old nettles are horrible. Young like this they are very good, though." Bridget was no longer surprised to hear her own voice in the garden, and she spoke much more freely than she usually did. It was she who suggested that it was time they went home, not Hilary, who usually took the initiative. She felt that for one day, the first day, she had drunk in enough of the strange atmosphere of the secret garden. Hilary would have liked to stay longer, but she remembered she was hungry and already late for tea.

SEVEN

A Quarrel

As they walked home, Hilary was planning out how much time they could spend in the garden and what measures they should take to keep it secret.

"You know, there's only one more week of term; we break up next week. It's with having Easter early this year, at the end of March. But we have one more weekend. Can you come this Saturday? We could take a picnic and stay all day. Take our homework too, perhaps."

"You won't tell your mother, will you?" asked Bridget nervously.

"What? About the garden? Oh, no! It is to be quite secret."

"You could say that we were going to Kensington Gardens."

Hilary did not mind keeping secrets from her mother, but to lie to her in order to conceal them was another matter. Yet it was a problem. Her mother was sure to ask

"Where are you going?" and then what should she answer?

"No," she said, dismissing Bridget's suggestion. "I could say . . . No, that wouldn't do. Or perhaps I could say we were . . . But that's a lie really too." Her face was screwed up into a frown as she grappled with the problem. "I shall tell her that I'm not going to tell her where we are going, and then I don't think she will ask."

Bridget did not seem entirely pleased with this solution and, although she said nothing about it, she did not intend to be so explicit with her aunt. But then her aunt was very different from Mrs. Toft, and she would probably have insisted on having her curiosity satisfied.

"In the holidays," said Bridget, "we shall be able to go there whenever we like."

"I'm going away," said Hilary, and she sounded disappointed. "We always go to my grandmother's for Easter. "We're going the very day the holidays start and staying for a fortnight, so there will only be a week left before next term starts." Although she usually looked forward to Easter at her grandmother's, she now felt very sorry to leave London almost as soon as they had discovered the garden. Bridget would be going there when she couldn't, and she felt jealous because it had been her discovery. By the time she came back Bridget and the garden would be thoroughly acquainted and she would be the stranger, and no closer to being Bridget's friend than she had been before.

"My grandmother is a great gardener, and I daresay she will give me lots of strange plants that we can put in the garden," she said to console herself. But it was not really very consoling. "You'd like to see her garden. I'm sure you wouldn't know the names of all the plants, because some of them come from the Alps and Granny smuggled them over herself." But all she could say did not make much difference. She was still jealous of Bridget, left in London.

But Bridget's thoughts were running in a different direction: alone, could she manage to climb into the garden?

"I suppose I could take a little stool and stand on it to get over the wall," she said.

Ah, Hilary had forgotten that! Bridget could not get on to the wall by herself.

"You couldn't leave a stool standing in Holland Walk, though. Anyone seeing it there'd soon think 'What a good idea' and come over too and the garden wouldn't be secret any more. Or someone would steal it, anyway."

"Oh, I wouldn't leave it standing there. I could lean over and lift it after me. Or if I couldn't do that I'd tie a string to it and pull it up."

"You'll look very funny walking through the streets with a great stool. It'll have to be quite big to be any use to you." Hilary was so eager to discourage Bridget that they were almost quarrelling and Bridget replied quite angrily now:

"That's silly. We've a stool that will just do, and it won't look so large when I'm carrying it because it's a camp stool and it folds up."

Hilary tried to be as provoking as she could by saying, "A camp stool!" in tones which suggested that only a fool would use that. "If it doesn't collapse when you stand on it, it certainly will if you try to jump off it! You'll just land on the paving stones with a nice lot of grazes and bruises and your beautiful neat clean clothes all dusty and dirty." Her voice was very sarcastic when she mentioned Bridget's neatness.

Bridget just said, "You don't want me to get into the garden," and withdrew into her shell and for all Hilary's denials and apologies remained silent and shut in. At Hereford Villas, when Mrs. Toft opened the door to them both, she noticed how pinched and silent Bridget looked.

"What have you been saying to Bridget?" she asked, when she could get her daughter alone into the kitchen, while Bridget was hanging up her coat.

"Nothing," said Hilary scowling. "Nothing much."

"You ought to have more sense! Here take this bread into the dining room."

Hilary returned in a moment for the cakes and jam.

"I had a plan," said her mother; "but I don't think it's worth trying now."

"She'll cheer up," said Hilary, kicking the kitchen door to and fro and watching its movement morosely.

"And stop kicking that door!" said Mrs. Toft. "You can take the tray. Don't drop it!"

When they sat down to tea Hilary was silent. She did not look at Bridget but instead rolled and unrolled the corner of the tablecloth that hung in her lap. Mrs. Toft did all the talking and gradually she began to bring Bridget out of her shell.

"I don't know what's come over you both," said Mrs. Toft. "There sits Hilary with the sulks, making a dirty rag out of my nice clean tablecloth"—Hilary dropped it hastily—"and not saying a word, which is most unlike her, as everybody knows. What is it? What is the 'something' that you've been doing after school?"

"Oh, just 'something'," said Hilary and she smiled because as soon as the question was asked she and Bridget had exchanged glances. They were fellow conspirators.

After this things got rather better and they seemed to forget the affair of the stool in the more important need to keep the garden secret. By the time they had finished tea they were both talking quite normally—Bridget a little, Hilary too much. Mrs. Toft decided that this was the most appropriate moment to propose her plan.

"We are going away next week to Lewes," she began, "to my mother's. Are you going anywhere for Easter, Bridget?"

"No," said Bridget and glanced at Hilary.

"You see, I was wondering if you would like to come too. David can't go this year, as he's going to a camp with the cadets, and my mother asked if Hilary would like to bring a friend."

She paused, and Bridget looked down in silence and then said, rather blushing and tongue-tied, "Would Hilary want me?"

"Oh, yes," burst in Hilary eagerly. "Oh, do come! You'd like it so much. I said you must meet Granny, didn't I? And she has a lovely garden." She could not add, "Perhaps you won't be able to get into the secret garden by yourself," but she thought it very hard, and almost willed Bridget to accept the invitation.

"I haven't spoken to Mrs. Sanders," said her mother,

"as I thought I'd ask you first to see what you thought of it. But as you say she hasn't made any other arrangements, I am sure she would let you. Would you like to come?"

Bridget looked at the tablecloth, and perhaps she would have liked to roll it up in her fingers, but she didn't. Instead she twisted her hands in and out of one another. It was not in her nature to jump at an invitation and, even if she would really have liked to accept it, her first instinct was to excuse herself. She preferred to run away and be by herself, and the idea of meeting a stranger, Hilary's grandmother, filled her with terror. On the other hand she dreaded the holidays spent at her aunt's house.

Even if she could get into the secret garden, she would probably have to spend much more time at home than she did during school. She could imagine how irritated her aunt would become at having her round the house. She would nag, nag, nag. How often it had happened before! Mr. Sanders would say, "Why can't you leave the child alone?"; but she couldn't. Perhaps Mrs. Sanders really thought she could nag Bridget into talking, and when she didn't succeed, as often as not she would lose her temper. Mr. Sanders quite liked Bridget, but then he did not see much of her. And sometimes he wished he had never agreed to give her a home because it made his wife so bad tempered.

So Bridget would gladly escape from that sort of a home for a fortnight. She screwed up her fingers in an effort to screw up the courage she needed to dare to accept the invitation.

Hilary watched her eagerly. If only she would come, it would be the very opportunity she needed. What with the garden and a fortnight's holiday together in the homely atmosphere of her grandmother's house, they would lay firmly the foundations of a friendship together. She could not understand why Bridget paused so long before accepting the invitation.

Mrs. Toft understood rather better why Bridget found it so difficult and embarrassing to make up her mind and she watched her a little anxiously. When Bridget turned to her at last she tried to reassure her with a smile. It was a catching smile, and Bridget smiled back and said diffidently, "I'd like to come, Mrs. Toft."

EIGHT

"Where did you live?"

On Saturday morning Bridget came round to Hereford Villas with some sandwiches in her satchel. The day was very fine and warm for the end of March and about the best they could have asked for spending in the garden. Mrs. Toft watched them start off down the road. Her expression was a little worried, and when she turned back into the house she said to herself, "I suppose it's all right to let them go off like that." She had accepted Hilary's statement about their destination, and had not asked any questions of her; but of herself she asked many. "Where are they going that it should be so important to keep it secret?" she thought.

They had walked a little way when Bridget said, "We must get some seeds." She had been preparing to say it for some time, but, when it came, it sounded very abrupt.

Hilary brushed the suggestion aside. "Oh! Let's just spend today exploring."

But Bridget had made her calculations. The seeds must be planted before they went to Lewes. They wouldn't be back in London till half way through April and by then the sowing season would be almost over. So time was short. She did not explain any of this to Hilary, but just said: "Have you got any money?"

Hilary had a shilling's pocket money which she usually laid out in sweets, but as her father gave it her on Saturday morning this week's was as yet unspent. Bridget also had a shilling.

"Oh, all right," said Hilary, giving in. "Where do you buy seeds?"

"Woolworth's," replied Bridget.

So they went to Woolworth's and had a good look at the seed counter to see what they would like to have. Bridget chose larkspur and nasturtiums.

"I don't like nasturtiums," objected Hilary; "they get all over little black things."

"They keep the black fly off other things," said Bridget and held on to her packet.

"Let's have pansies," suggested Hilary.

"They won't flower till next year."

"Oh, why not?"

"They're biennials."

"Oh." Hilary digested the fact. "What about snapdragons?"

"They're biennials too."

"Everything's biennials that I want! What about sunflowers?"

"They're annuals."

"So we can't have them either?"

"Oh, yes. Annuals flower in one year."

"Ah, good. What else?"

Bridget chose mignonette and poppies, and blue cornflowers but Hilary found a packet of cornflowers of mixed colors, so they had that instead. Hilary chose schizanthus because she thought the picture on the packet looked so fancy and delicate, and they completed their purchases with French marigolds. Hilary was sorry to see all her money go and said so. "Couldn't we buy some of the seeds when we get back?" she asked, eyeing the sweet counter.

"They ought to be planted now," said Bridget. She didn't care about sweets. Her whole mind was set on the garden and she could hardly wait to see the seeds that she would have sown spring up in the new dug earth. There would already be little plants when they came back after Easter, if they sowed the seeds now.

Hilary was reading the instructions on the backs of the packets. "This one says 'March to April'." It'll still be April when we come back."

"They'd be better planted now," said Bridget stubbornly. She did not argue or explain, but before her stubborn determination Hilary gave in, and they left Woolworth's with the eight packets of seeds.

Hilary soon forgot the sweets and she talked happily until they turned the corner of Holland Walk, when she changed her voice to a whisper and said, "If we are to come here often we mustn't attract attention. Perhaps it would be better if we talked as little as possible in Holland Walk itself."

So they walked circumspectly and kept their eyes open and their mouths shut until they came to the door in the wall. Bridget had not seen this before because of the diversion of the passing tramp, and the notice had the opposite effect on her to that it had had on Hilary.

Whoever enters here never comes out again.

"D'you think it's safe?"

"Why, of course. Some fool wrote that up for a joke."

But the mysterious warning had unnerved Bridget. "Perhaps we'd better not go in after all," she suggested falteringly.

"Why ever not? We went in before, didn't we, and we're still alive? You don't want to give up the secret garden do you?"

"N-no."

"Well, come on. And after we've bought all those seeds!"

Once inside the garden Bridget's fears lessened, and soon she had forgotten them altogether. They followed the same path as before through the shrubbery, out by the urn, and across the lawn into the enclosed garden with little hedges.

"What about that part over there?" said Hilary, pointing to the left. Bridget led the way, skirting the lawn to a place where a rose garden had once been arranged facing the shrubbery. There were a number of pergolas and bits of trellis work, and amongst the tangled mass some standard roses could still be seen with their tall stems trained straight.

"These will all have run to briars," said Bridget. "Unless someone has come to prune them secretly, as in the story in my book."

"That won't have happened here," said Hilary. "At least, I doubt it. Who'd come?"

Bridget bent to examine the leaves and said, "No, these are all briars. They've seven leaves apiece."

Beyond the roses were some lilacs and laburnums, not yet out, of course, and beyond them the garden wall marked the end of the territory.

"They won't have come to any harm," said Bridget pointing to the lilacs and laburnums. "They should make a fine show."

The ground beneath the lilacs and laburnums was overrun with ivy, and in their midst rose a curious mass, perhaps about seven feet high, completely swathed in a pall of ivy. They went towards it and lifted aside the curtain of ivy leaves. It revealed inside a little summerhouse, built of wood, with seats running round the walls. In the middle, standing alone, was a strange piece of iron machinery, much rusted and broken, with a number of cog wheels at one end. Bridget shrank back.

"What is it?" she asked. It was dark inside the summerhouse behind the curtain of ivy and the piece of machinery looked sinister. Bridget remembered the writing on the door and foreboding filled her again.

But Hilary went forward in frank curiosity, and then she laughed. "It's the post of a tennis net! Look, here are the cranks to tighten the net."

Bridget smiled with relief and said, "So it is."

"I suppose they played tennis on that lawn that was. It must be quite large." Hilary lifted the curtain of ivy and they looked back towards the lawn. Once a vista had been planned from the summerhouse, so that you looked under arches of roses now tumbledown and overgrown with festoons of new briar, across the lawn to the urn with its circle of seats and the shrubbery behind.

"It would have made a pretty view then," said Hilary, reconstructing it in her mind's eye.

"I like it now."

"All wild? Yes, it's more exciting. It's awfully big, you know, for a London garden."

"Your mother said these were country houses once, before this was London at all. She was telling me about them, when we went to Kew, you know. That was why they had big gardens, she said."

"Why, yes, come to think of it," said Hilary, "it does look an oldish house. It was probably built while it still was country round here. Just think of it! Fields and farms all over Ladbroke Grove, and Kensington just a village, perhaps."

They stood pensively, thinking themselves back a century or more until they had imagined away all the London which spread for many miles to the north, west, and south of them, and they were in a garden in the country.

Like a fossil in a lump of rock the old garden, a remnant of a past world, was embedded in the growth of London. The town had marched on, sprawling over hills and clotting up the valleys, and the garden had been forgotten behind its high walls, a little, unchanged fragment of country life.

"Of course, it can't have been bombed so very long ago," said Hilary. "But somehow it feels as if it had been deserted ever since London caught up with it and it was cut off from the country. Do you know what I mean?"

"I think so. It doesn't belong to our present-day London."

"Yes. With these high walls round, it can't see what's happened. It lives in the past. And we're like the children with the amulet, who've stepped back into the past and found it."

Still musing, they left the summerhouse and pushed their way through the tangle of briars. Bridget led the way back into the part with the hedges.

"There's a greenhouse here," she said, "or was." Against a stretch of south wall were the traces of the greenhouse. All the glass and most of the woodwork had disappeared; there remained a patch of weathered whitewash on the south wall and the low containing wall from which the roof of glass had once sloped up. The main bar of the framework was still in place, sloping up to the top of the whitewashed patch. There was broken glass in the nettles, and broken pots inside.

"Fancy its all having gone," said Hilary, touching the one bar as they entered under it. "Do you think people stole the woodwork for firewood, or that it just rotted away?"

"I don't know. Look at all these bits of pots. There isn't one whole one left."

"I'd like to plant some of our seeds here. It would cheer it up a bit. Somehow it seems more miserable and desolate here than anywhere else."

"It'll all be nettles soon," objected Bridget, pointing to where the little nettles were springing thickly along the wall. "They're even coming up between the bricks."

A path paved with bricks ran the length of the greenhouse. Perhaps there had been shelves on either side, but there was nothing left of them now. Round the walls, partly hidden in weeds, ran some old hot water pipes by which the place had once been heated. Bridget began to pull the weeds away from them to see where they came from. She carefully avoided disturbing some creepers whose thick, twisted trunks had been trained against the wall. "Though they're dead, I think," she said.

"What are they?" asked Hilary.

"Vines, I imagine."

"Fancy!" said Hilary. "I had no idea what a vine looked like."

"We used to grow them, where we lived."

"Where was that?" asked Hilary, suddenly interested. "Was that when your parents were alive?"

Bridget ignored the question, and so after a slight pause Hilary repeated it. "Where did you live then, where you grew the vines?"

Instead of answering, Bridget exclaimed, "Look!", but with such an obviously forced display of excitement that Hilary was not distracted.

"What at?" she said impatiently.

"The pipes go through the wall."

"Well, what of it?"

"There must be a boiler house on the other side," explained Bridget, rather feebly.

"A boiler house!" exclaimed Hilary. "How exciting!" She began to get interested. She did not forget that she wanted to find out where Bridget used to live, but she could ask about that another time. "Where can this boiler house be?" she said. "We must find it."

Bridget emerged from the greenhouse and said, "There's a door here in the wall."

Hilary followed her, and kicked away the mass of weeds which almost hid the door, and put her hand to the latch. But the door would open only an inch or two towards them, and then would not budge.

"It's all these weeds that are blocking it," said Bridget. "We'll have to clear them away properly."

Hilary stung her hands on the nettles and scratched them too, on some brambles, in her haste to clear the door. All the same, it would open only about nine inches.

"We can get through that," said Hilary, and forced her fat body into the opening. Something caught. Hilary squeeze and pulled. There was a tearing sound and she was through with a three-cornered tear in her coat.

"Oh, there's a nail," she said. "My mother will be so pleased. Wait a minute and I'll get it out." She pulled off her shoe and, using the heel as a hammer, she flattened the offending nail against the door jamb. "That will be all right now. Come on. Sometimes it is an advantage to be thin," she added, grinning at Bridget.

Bridget carefully insinuated herself through the crack, without tearing anything, and indeed without rubbing and dirtying any of her clothes.

"Here's your boiler house," said Hilary.

Built in the corner of the walls on this side was a longish shed or outhouse with two doors. One was at ground level, but the other, nearest the greenhouse, was reached down a few steps, though it was impossible to see them at first as the hollow was completely filled with dead leaves.

"Oh, let's have lunch, before we start another clearance job," said Hilary. So they went to the circle of seats round the urn and unpacked the sandwiches.

It was a sunny spot, and the day was warm for the time of year. They ate in a comfortable silence looking out into the garden, each one making plans for the future they would spend there.

Suddenly something happened which they were quite unprepared for. There were footsteps behind them from the shrubbery and they swung round in terror to find an old woman standing there. They froze. Their first instinct was to leap into the bushes, but it was obviously too late. They had been seen, and anyway they would have had to leave the open packet of sandwiches on the seat behind them, a too obvious evidence of their presence. So they just sat and stared, their sandwiches half way to their mouths. In the half second that they sat there a hundred thoughts passed through their minds. Was the house after all inhabited? Would the old lady turn them out in anger? Perhaps hand them over to the police for trespassing?

"It's a nice day, isn't it?" said the old lady, smiling amiably.

Well, that did not sound like an angry owner. Hilary found her tongue and said, "Yes, isn't it? Warm, for March."

The old lady had a bunch of violets in her hand and she showed it them. “There are quite a lot out,” she said. “It’s the warm weather that is bringing them on.”

“Oh, yes. Aren’t they pretty?” said Hilary, conversationally.

The old lady stooped to pick another by the path and said, “A queer place this. No one’s lived here for years.”

"Yes," said Hilary. "It's very queer. No one lives here at all, do they?"

"No, not since it was bombed, and that was years ago. But I won't interrupt your lunch," she added, and wandered off, stooping and picking violets as she went.

They watched her go, still a little shaken by the shock and clutching their half-eaten sandwiches. When she was out of earshot Hilary whispered, "How did *she* get in? She couldn't climb over the wall."

Bridget did not reply, and they continued to watch the figure of the old lady moving amongst the bushes and ivy until she had disappeared in the direction of the house.

"There must be another way in down there," said Hilary, and stuffed the remainder of her sandwich into her mouth. "I'm just going to see where she goes," she added, and began to follow the old lady at a discreet distance. After some minutes she returned and said, "There's some sort of yard by the side of the house. I only caught a glimpse of it, because she shut the door behind her, and bolted it, too. I don't think she wants just anyone coming in here any more than we do, which is lucky isn't it? Anyway, let's find some more secluded spot to finish our lunch."

They found a place under the apple trees in the further part of the garden where, when Hilary had stamped down the undergrowth, they could sit down and be entirely hidden from anyone who might come there.

"Well," said Hilary when they were established. "We shall have to be more careful if we are to keep this place secret. She mayn't be the only person who comes here."

Bridget asked in a hushed voice, "Do you think many people come here?"

"No, I don't think *many* people come here, and I don't see why we shouldn't come here as often as we like without their seeing us. We couldn't find a more secret garden, I'm sure. And, I know what, we can build ourselves some lairs inside it, which will be completely secret. We can hide ourselves very well here."

"We can't plant anything or they'll soon find us out."

"I don't see why we shouldn't. Why, if we planted them here where we are now, no one would see them. They'd think it was just weeds all the way through."

"I thought you wanted to plant things in the old greenhouse."

"Hmm, yes," said Hilary thoughtfully. "I still don't see why we shouldn't. If we get rid of those nettles we could plant lots of other things that might have seeded themselves naturally, in a sort of natural profusion, not one by one like flowers in a formal garden."

"Yes, I suppose one could."

"Anyway the chief thing is that we can't just walk about in the middle of the lawn where anyone coming in can see us at first glance. We must go about carefully and not be seen."

When they had finished their lunch, they decided to start planting their seeds. Bridget had brought a trowel and fork from home to do the job. It seemed best to clear the ground where they had been sitting, as it was well screened by the undergrowth. The ground had not been dug for so long that it was very difficult to break up and was matted through and through with the roots of things.

They came the next afternoon to go on with the work and did not finish putting the seeds in until the following week, after school.

"Now, let's hope it rains while we're away," said Bridget.

"Well, in London, anyway. But I hope we get some fine weather in Lewes."

NINE

Plants from the Country

The holiday at Lewes passed very quietly. Mr. Toft was there for the Easter weekend and then he went back to London, leaving Mrs. Toft with Hilary and Bridget and Mrs. Fisher, Mrs. Toft's mother. The weather was very changeable, sunny and blowy one day and raining torrents the next, but there seemed to be plenty to do whatever the weather was like. Mrs. Fisher's house was old and large with a little spiral back staircase and a great many attics which were not used at all, or only as boxrooms. These attics were wonderful places to live in on rainy days, and they had some of the character of the secret garden. No one went there, nor had been there, it would seem, for ages. There one might sit by the hour undisturbed and read some of the hundreds of books that Mrs. Fisher had collected over a lifetime.

But despite the attractions of the attics, Hilary and Bridget spent most of their time out of doors when the weather was possible, and even when most people would have thought it impossible.

"It really is a wonder," said Mrs. Toft, "that neither of you has caught a cold, the number of times you've got soaked through. And that does not mean you're not to be more careful, for I don't know what I should say to Bridget's aunt if she died of pneumonia."

But she was glad to see them go out such a lot and, whenever there was a gleam of sunshine, she encouraged them to make the most of it.

"That's the pity," Mrs. Toft said to her mother, one day when the two girls were out, "of living in London. Children should be out in the fresh air much more often than they can be there. Bridget's looking much less pasty-faced since she came here. I do wish we had a larger garden at Hereford Villas, though of course that's asking for the impossible. Life might be a little quieter too, for me. Hilary's such a noisy girl to have about the house all the time."

"She seems to be much quieter than she used to be," said her grandmother, smiling.

"Ah," said Mrs. Toft, "that's Bridget's influence, and very glad of it I am. They make a strange pair, don't they? Bridget's not the sort of girl that I would ever have imagined Hilary would make friends with."

"She comes from the country originally, doesn't she? She seems to be very interested in gardens, and knows a lot about it too."

Mrs. Toft had already told her mother a good deal about Bridget that she had learnt from Mrs. Sanders and had never told Hilary, and now she filled in the gaps.

"I can hardly believe all you tell me," Mrs. Fisher said "Bridget's a quiet child, certainly, and a shy one, but what you say makes her sound positively odd. I'd not think it from what I've seen of her."

"You should have seen her at first. I hope this change in her will be a permanent one."

"By the way, where are they going to put in all these plants they have been asking me for? Have Bridget's people got a big garden?"

"They've been asking you for plants?" exclaimed Mrs. Toft, much surprised. "What on earth for? No, the Sanders have an even smaller garden than ours. What can they be up to?"

"Oh dear, I see I shouldn't have told you!" said Mrs. Fisher, very sorry for what she had said. "I thought you would know all about it. They didn't tell me it was a secret. You won't breathe a word about it, will you, my dear?"

"That's asking rather a lot. They may be up to all kinds of mischief, and get themselves into real trouble."

"Nonsense, they'll not get themselves into trouble, nor do anything they shouldn't, I'll be bound. They're both sensible girls, and good ones too, at heart. Did you never keep a secret from me? Don't you go butting into it. You'll know all about it, all in good time."

Mrs. Fisher, like all grandmothers, was more tolerant of the doings of her grandchildren than their own mothers were. Having herself brought up a family successfully, she thought that her daughter's fears and worries were vastly exaggerated. Eventually she persuaded Mrs. Toft that the secret could only be quite harmless, and not a word should should be said about it.

The day before they left, Bridget and Hilary carefully packed their plants. There were seedlings of some of the biennials that Hilary had wanted to grow from seed: the pansies and snapdragons, together with sweet peas and lavender and sweet-williams. Besides these, there were some roots of sedum and of Mrs. Fisher's specialties, astrantia and acanthus.

"You won't tell Mummy about these, will you, Granny?" asked Hilary.

"Oh, no," said her grandmother. "That's a secret among the three of us."

And Mrs. Toft carefully avoided noticing or remarking on the contents of the paper carriers and satchels which they took home with them, so that the two of them thought that nothing had been suspected.

The plants could not be kept out of the earth for very long, so the first thing Bridget and Hilary did, after tea on the same day as they got back, was to go round to the secret garden to put them in. They took with them some small garden tools.

"It's a pity we can't take anything big," said Hilary; "but we'd have to carry them to and fro the whole time, as my father would want to use them in our garden at home in between. And if we were always carrying spades and things about, people would soon discover our secret garden."

They arrived at the garden and climbed over the wall without mishap. No one was around. They made straight for the greenhouse, where they had decided to put most of their things in.

A great change had come over the garden while they had been away. They caught a glimpse of the lawn through the shrubbery. It was green and lush and the grass stood high, but they avoided crossing it in case they should be seen.

"Why, there's something with pink flowers there in the ivy," whispered Hilary.

"It's flowering currant," said Bridget.

But when they opened the door in the wall by the greenhouse, they saw what a real change had taken place. They remembered this part of the garden as a place full of dead sticks grown grimy and still standing there from last summer. Now it was a sea of green.

"How the nettles have grown!" exclaimed Bridget.

"You can't see the little hedges or the paths now," said Hilary, as she made her way out along one of the latter. The tall nettles bowed over from either side and met in the middle, and she had to push them away with her skirt before she could walk through. And she stung her legs all over just the same. From above, one could see the tops of the hedges, the brownish yellow-green of box amongst the blue-green of nettles which stood as high as them on either side.

In the greenhouse the nettles had run riot too, and they were very dense along the wall where they had planned to put their plants.

"We can't clear those," said Hilary. "Let's look for somewhere else."

So they wandered about the garden, but everywhere

was the same. It was hard to identify the place where they had sown their seeds, for new nettles had sprung there too. The rose garden was more than ever a tangle of sharp-thorned briars, through which they could not pass to reach the summerhouse. New shoots showed bright and green, twining and intertwining to make an impenetrable thicket.

"I supoose the greenhouse is the best place after all," said Hilary resignedly, as she licked the blood off her scratched hand. So they returned there.

Hilary stood looking at the crop of nettles in a bemused manner, not knowing what to do, but Bridget looked in her satchel and produced an old pair of rubber gloves.

"You think of everything!" exclaimed Hilary, and then added, as Bridget had already knelt down and started work, "But what can I do?"

Bridget pointed out a patch where there were no nettles, but other weeds instead, and Hilary set to work there. "Next time I must see if I can bring some gloves too," she said.

"It's a good thing," said Bridget, "that the nettles are still fairly small."

"Fairly small!" exclaimed Hilary, who had just stung her hand on one. "They seem jolly big to me."

"Oh, they're tiny, now, really. They'll grow quite as tall as us before long. Then it would be impossible to get them out with these silly little forks. As it is, I don't think I can get out all these old roots."

It was certainly hard work and presently Hilary stood up to stretch her back. She looked out into the garden

and back to the patch they had cleared, which seemed very small by comparison. She looked up at the white-washed wall of the greenhouse and then exclaimed, "Why, it's not dead!"

It was one of the old brown vines against the wall that she referred to, and she leant over closer to examine it. "It's putting out little shoots and tendrils," she said.

Bridget stood up and came over to have a look at it. "Yes, it is a vine, and it's alive," she said.

Hilary had scarcely thought again about Bridget's strange evasive behavior on the first occasion, when they had seen the vine. She was reminded of it now, and she looked speculatively at Bridget.

"You say you used to grow lots of vines?" she asked.

Bridget was well aware of what was going on in Hilary's mind. A few moments elapsed and Hilary was about to continue her interrogation when Bridget suddenly swung round and said defiantly, "Yes, we did, in Guernsey, if you want to know!" Then she turned quickly away and Hilary was surprised to see the color mounting in her neck, while her whole cheek, as much of her face as she could see, suddenly reddened. But she was not going to be put off by this.

"Oh, I didn't know you lived in Guernsey," she remarked as casually as possible. "What was it like living in the Channel Isles?"

To this she got no answer.

"Now I see," Hilary went on, "why you know French so well. They talk French there, don't they?"

Bridget muttered, "Yes."

"Did your parents talk French at home?"

At the mention of her parents Bridget flinched, and muttered hastily, "No. No, they didn't."

After a slight pause, Hilary took up her questioning again. "I do wonder," she said, "what it was like living on a little island like that. Was it much warmer there than in England?"

"Yes . . . I don't know."

"I mean, did you grow the grapes out of doors, or in a greenhouse?"

"Er . . . yes."

"Out of doors?"

"Er . . . no."

"So you grew them in a greenhouse, like these. Do you think these will have any grapes on them? I say, wouldn't it be wonderful if they did!"

"I don't suppose they'll ripen if there are any," said Bridget, relieved to find the conversation had taken a turn away from Guernsey.

"But wouldn't it be wonderful if they did! Don't you like grapes?"

"Not all that much. One gets bored with them, like anything else."

"Bored? But then I suppose you're used to them. We didn't have any during the War. Were you in Guernsey during the War?"

It seemed to cost Bridget a considerable struggle to answer this question. She went very red again, and at length said, "No."

Hilary had an uncanny feeling that this was a lie, and she could not understand why it had been told. Since she seemed to be getting nowhere with her questions, she picked up a trowel and joined in the work.

They did not speak again until they were about to leave, and then they talked about other things, plants and nettles and the garden. Bridget seemed to want to forget that Guernsey had been mentioned. Hilary began to feel that she had been unkind in pressing her questions, but she was still devoured by curiosity and more puzzled than ever by Bridget's behavior.

TEN

Two Bridgets

Hilary did not mention Guernsey again to Bridget but when she got home she spoke to her mother.

"I didn't know Bridget lived in Guernsey."

"No?" said her mother. "Did she tell you?"

"Yes," said Hilary; and then, after a pause, "Did you know?"

"Mrs. Sanders told me."

"Oh. Did she live there a long time?"

"She was born and bred there, you know."

"And when did she leave?"

"After the War, when the Germans had gone."

So Bridget had lied. She had felt it before, but now she knew.

"The Germans?" she asked. "What were they doing in Guernsey?"

"During the war the Germans invaded and occupied the Channel Islands, Guernsey included. Now I must go and get supper." And Mrs. Toft snapped shut the book she had been reading when Hilary came in and went out to the kitchen. Hilary had to accept this as a hint that the subject was closed. She still wondered why Bridget had said she had not lived in Guernsey during the War, but she said nothing more about it.

It rained that night and the next day. Hilary saw the rain in the morning with satisfaction; this would give their plants a chance against the nettles.

When the weather permitted them to visit the garden again, they found that the plants had taken root lustily and were quite able to fight for the ground they grew on. But the two girls had also to see to the seeds that they had sown. If these were to have a chance, the nettles which already submerged them must be removed, and quickly. Otherwise the seedlings would be choked out of life, like the seeds in the Bible that fell amongst the thistles, as Hilary said. It was a painful and weary job and Hilary did not enjoy it. She was clumsy at pulling out the nettles and brought out the seedlings too, but Bridget was quick and skilled, and what was more, she knew the plants from one another and which were the weeds to be rooted out.

"I don't know how you know which are which," Hilary complained with admiration. "They all look alike to me."

"They are alike when they are very small. Lots of plants come up with two little leaves like mustard and cress, weeds and flowers as well. But soon they get their own special shape of leaves."

"Even then they look much the same to me. Is this one of our plants?"

"That? No, that's ground ivy!"

"Then I'll pull it up. And this?"

"Leave it. But you can pull that one up; it's groundsel."

"Oh, I knew that. My aunt gives it to her canary." Hilary was very pleased that there was one she knew.

When at last the patch was cleared they could see their own little seedlings growing in the places they had been sown in, the sunflowers at the back, and then the larkspur, and all the others according to the size they would be when grown, so that the smallest, the French marigolds, came at the front. To Bridget the little plants were more precious than gold, and Hilary, too was excited to see how the little hard dry seeds had come to life and pushed their green leaves through the earth.

"We could get some more," she said. "It's still April and the packets said April was all right. There's such a lot of room here," she said waving her arm over the sighing, whispering mass of nettles that reached to their knees. "Are there some other annuals that we didn't get?"

So they went to Woolworth's and chose love-in-the-mist and clarkia and bartonia aurea and eschscholtzia.

"What a name!" exclaimed Hilary. "How do you get it all into your mouth at once?"

Term began, and often, after school, they would spend half an hour in the garden. With practice Bridget became more agile and could mount the wall without assistance. Nevertheless, they usually went together. In school also they were usually seen together to the consternation and mirth of their schoolfellows. The effect of Miss Mills's exhortation to be kind had entirely worn off by now, and these girls were peeved by Bridget's refusal or inability to be communicative with them. They often took occasion to embarrass her in little cruel ways, though they would have denied this indignantly if they had been openly accused of it. Bridget was only too conscious of these petty persecutions; they made her miserable, and just as the term before she had always moved in Catherine's shadow for protection, now she attached herself to Hilary. In school she was a very different girl from the one who had spent the holidays in the old house at Lewes. She was her old self again—the thin white-faced girl who flinched when she was asked a question, who never smiled or spoke.

But in the garden the brighter, more cheerful Bridget re-emerged. If it was she who followed Hilary around in school time, as soon as they were over the wall the position was reversed. Then, quietly but with practical good sense, Bridget took the lead. It was she who had the best ideas and who decided what was to be done. And it was she who accomplished the greater amount of work that was involved. Although she had a willing laborer in Hilary, she had a rather impractical one, and one who quickly tired when things went slowly, and who would break off for a rest and start talking while Bridget slogged on.

The next work that they undertook in the garden was to construct a lair under the apple trees, now pink and white with blossom, so that they could reach their plot of flowers. The nettles and other undergrowth and grown almost to their shoulders and through this they cut a passage with a carefully concealed entry. It was grueling work and painful too, because of the nettles. Hilary took many prolonged rests while Bridget worked on. At last Hilary's conscience smote her.

"Look here," she said, "you *must* take a rest. Let me put my nose to the grindstone and see how far I can get."

So Bridget straightened her back and Hilary took her place and the kitchen scissors and worked hard for some time. But presently she tired, and looked around. And when she looked around she saw that Bridget was not there. So she stood up and looked over the top of the nettles, but Bridget was not to be seen.

In the garden they did not call to one another for fear they should be overheard, but instead, when there was need of it, they mewed softly like cats to catch one another's attention. Hilary mewed now, but received no reply. She crept over to the greenhouse.

"Miaow!" she called. And then "Miaow!" again a little louder. Then she listened to the silence. Over the wall in the shrubbery she heard the rustling of leaves, a scraping and some thudding noises.

"Miaow!" she ventured again, tentatively.

"Miaow!" came the answer. Hilary was quickly at the door in the wall and found Bridget on the other side with a large fork and spade on her shoulder and a pair of shears on the ground at her feet.

"I thought we might find something in there," she said, triumphantly, pointing at the shed next to the boiler house. "And then I kept on forgetting to look when we were here."

"These will be invaluable!" exclaimed Hilary and picked up the shears.

"They are very blunt," said Bridget. "But we could get them sharpened."

This discovery halved their labors, and soon after this they completed the lair to which the passage led. It was completely hidden from all sides; inside it was spacious enough so that one could sit or lie at ease. When the weather was fine they would often come there after tea, and do their homework, and on weekends they would lie there concealed whole mornings or afternoons.

In time they started on a second lair with a hidden entry from the first lair, so that they would be able to retire further into the jungle should their first hiding place be discovered. By now the apple blossom had fallen, and the nettles and their hiding place were all flecked with white. The petals lodged in their hair when they went there so that they looked as if they had come from a wedding.

All this time Hilary had not mentioned Guernsey again, nor the lie that Bridget had told her. But often she watched Bridget and wondered what went on in her mind and longed to know what mystery she was concealing. It was chiefly at school that she watched her thus, when the old silent Bridget was present.

In a math lesson one afternoon she was watching her in this way. That lunch hour some of the others had teased Bridget with particular cruelty, taunting her and trying to make her talk to them. Hilary had come quickly to her aid, but already there was a pinched look of terror on Bridget's face, and it was there still. They had been given some sums, and Miss Hammond was walking up and down the rows of desks looking over their shoulders to see how they were getting on. Hilary was not doing any sums at all; she had fallen into a reverie watching Bridget, over the other side of the room. Their desks were far separated and three broad sunbeams fell across the room between them, in which myriads of specks of chalk dust danced and drifted endlessly. Miss Hammond wandered amongst the desks and looked over Bridget's shoulder. Bridget was not doing any sums either. She bit her pen and stared fixedly at the paper before her. Her mind was blank of all but the misery of being there.

Hilary saw Miss Hammond lean over Bridget's shoulder

and rest her hand on the edge of the desk. She was talking to her in a low explanatory voice. From where she sat Hilary could see part of Bridget's face; she seemed to twitch slightly when she was spoken to and she did not look up, but stared at the paper as if there was no one behind her. When she had finished her explanation Miss Hammond leaned lower on her arm so that her head was level with Bridget's, as if to catch the words she did not speak.

Hilary heard her ask: "Do you understand that, Bridget?"

After waiting a few moments for some answer, she patiently began again from the beginning to explain the sum. Some of the other girls seemed to find this very amusing, and exchanged glances.

When she had finished her explanation, Miss Hammond said as kindly as she could, hiding her impatience, "If you understand this, Bridget, just say yes. I only want to know that you understand what you are trying to do."

Bridget must have said yes to this, though Hilary did not hear it, for Miss Hammond straightened up and said: "Good. I will come back presently and see if you have been able to do it. Hilary Toft, get on with your work."

So Hilary had to turn back to her sums.

After school, when she expected Bridget to be waiting for her, she found that she had slipped through her fingers and gone amongst the first. It was a long time since she had slipped off like this without a word and Hilary was hurt and puzzled.

ELEVEN

The Truant

The next day Bridget was absent.

"She must have felt ill yesterday afternoon," said Hilary to herself. It was an easy explanation. If she had been feeling sick it was not surprising that she had not been up to the sums. "Why ever didn't she tell Miss Hammond?" thought Hilary. She was a little hurt that she had not told her, Hilary. "I could have taken her home," she thought. Nevertheless it explained things, that she should have been feeling ill.

After school Hilary thought she would go and call at Banbury Terrace and find out what was wrong with Bridget. Perhaps Mrs. Sanders would say, "Oh it's a slight cold," or perhaps, "A stomach upset. Do go up and see her, Hilary. Can you stay to tea? It would cheer her up a great deal."

On the other hand it might be something serious. "I ought to take some flowers" was the next thought. "Shall I go home and pick some marigolds?" Then she remembered the old lady picking violets in the garden. They had never picked anything in the garden themselves but now was the opportunity. Hilary turned up Holland Walk and climbed into the garden.

The violets were over. Hilary explored the shrubbery for them but there were none. Across the lawn, the ivy-covered summerhouse was banked round with the purple and white and yellow of lilac and laburnum. Hilary wondered if she should pick some of it. At first it seemed an excellent idea but then she realized that it would excite comment. Mrs. Sanders would ask where an armful of lilac came from. So she went through the door into the other part of the garden to see what else she could find. She picked a handful of pansies and other flowers from those they had planted in the old greenhouse.

Then she went to their lair. Why not visit it, since she was in the garden? There might already be some flowers there too.

She stepped into the concealed entrance of the passage, and then she heard something move inside. She froze. Who was there? Who could have found their place? She was half frightened and half angry too, that someone should have the presumption to make use of *their* hiding place, that *they* had cut with such labor. She stood still and fuming. But what should she do? Slip away unseen? But she might be seen anyway. Go on and find out who it was? And what should she say then? But she decided to go on and have it out, so she stepped boldly into the lair.

There was no one there. So their second lair was discovered too. Hilary was really angry. She entered the second opening; and then suddenly a little voice from inside the further lair said, "Hullo, Hilary."

And there was Bridget.

Hilary sat down very suddenly on the ground and said, "I thought you were ill."

In half a second a great many thoughts can pass through one's mind. Hilary's first thought on seeing Bridget was that she *had* been ill, and then got better and come out. "Fancy Mrs. Sanders letting her get up and go out so soon. My mother wouldn't," she thought. But even as she thought this the real explanation dawned on her. So Bridget was playing truant.

Bridget offered no comment on her remark but sat down too, facing her, and began to pull to pieces a leaf she had in her hand.

"I was going to go round and ask after you," said Hilary. She began to feel rather angry that she had so nearly made a fool of herself and wasted so many kindly sentiments on the supposed invalid, who might well have confided in her.

"You ought to be jolly glad I came here first, instead," she said.

Bridget had looked up in horror, realizing how easily Hilary, quite accidentally, might have betrayed her truancy to her aunt. Mrs. Sanders would then have a real excuse for being angry and she was angry often enough without having any excuse. To tell the truth, Bridget was more frightened of her aunt than of any of the school bullies.

"I was going to bring you these flowers," said Hilary. "I thought you were ill."

Bridget plucked another leaf and began to dismember it. She said nothing. And Hilary did not know what to say next. She had never known anyone to play truant before.

"I wonder if any of them do," she thought, running through her classmates and acquaintances. "Perhaps it is more common than one thinks. But why?" For her own part she had never for a moment desired to do it. She liked school because there were plenty of people to talk to and to get into pickles with. She liked the lessons too, for she was a clever girl and enjoyed exercising her wits. Of course there were some she disliked, but it would never have entered her head to stay away simply to miss a singing or a geography lesson. In fact, if ever she was ill, what irked her most was that she was missing something that others were doing, and that they were probably not missing her, but getting on very nicely without her. So she could not understand why Bridget should have done this.

After a few minutes' consideration which got her no

nearer an answer, Hilary asked, "What made you play truant?"

Bridget began to twiddle a root that stuck out of the ground, as if it were her sole object in life to get it out. "They're horrid," she mumbled, pouting.

"Who are horrid?" asked Hilary, leaning close to catch the mumbled words.

"Everybody," said Bridget, not raising her head.

"Everybody? Am I horrid?"

"No, not you." She still mumbled and was engrossed in her root.

"Not me. Then Catherine? She's not horrid to you, is she?"

"No, not Catherine."

"Not Catherine. And what about Miss Hammond? Was she being 'horrid' to you yesterday?"

"She goes on and on, questioning me. Why can't she leave me alone?"

"But she only wanted to make sure you understood. It's not as if she was the inquisition, or something, trying to get information out of you, is it, now?"

"I don't know. I wish she'd leave me alone."

Hilary thought. It was still a puzzle to her.

"Oh, cheer up!" she said. "I know the other girls are horrid. But why do you bother about them? They won't do you any harm."

Bridget made no reply to this so she went on, "I wouldn't care tuppence for them. They're fools. Take no notice of them."

Still no response.

"I'd pull all their noses if I were you," said Hilary, "except Miss Hammond, of course. I'll do it for you if you like," she added generously. This course appealed to her, but it did not appeal to Bridget, who still pulled at the root.

"What are you going to do tomorrow? Will you come to school?"

"I don't know."

"Oh, I should. I'll look after you. No one shall bully you."

"All right," mumbled Bridget, more to settle Hilary than because she intended to.

"What'll you do? I mean, you must bring a note if you've been absent."

"I'll write one."

"But it must come from your aunt, you know."

"I'll write one from my aunt."

This shocked Hilary. "That's very wrong," she said. "Suppose you were found out?"

"I've never been before."

"You've done it before?" It was surprising enough that Bridget should play truant once, but that she should be a habitual truant player was quite astounding. "What, here, at school?"

"Not here, but before—at the other school I went to."

Hilary was somewhat reassured to learn that it had not been going on under her very nose. "I don't think you should write a note from your aunt, all the same. It's most dishonest. Forgery, I suppose. Why, you might even be tried for it!"

But Bridget said nothing and Hilary could think of no other way out. Then another thought struck her.

"Have you had nothing to eat?" she asked.

"No," said Bridget.

This really appalled Hilary, for she was a girl with a healthy appetite and could not imagine going without her lunch. "You must be starved. Aren't you hungry?"

"I suppose so."

"I should think so." Hilary was thoughtful for a moment and then she said, "You know, we could keep some food here in the garden. It would be useful sometimes." She was not really laying plans for Bridget to play truant again, but she felt it best to provide against the contingency.

"You needn't worry about me. I don't mind," said Bridget.

"Oh, but it would often be useful to have some food here."

"It would go bad, or dry, or something."

"Some things wouldn't do, certainly. Bread would go dry. But there are some things that keep."

"Biscuits," volunteered Bridget, to whom the scheme was beginning to appeal.

"Biscuits are rationed," objected Hilary. "We couldn't buy them without ration books."

"We could get biscuits from home. I could. Couldn't you?" Bridget now urged it, having thoroughly fallen in with the idea.

"Perhaps," said Hilary; "I'll try." Then she rose and asked, "Don't you want to go home now? You must want your tea."

"I suppose so." Bridget would have liked to put off the dreaded return home to her aunt, but she could think of no excuses.

Hilary picked up the bunch of flowers.

"What are you going to do with those?" asked Bridget.

"Would you like them?"

"What could I do with them? Better leave them here."

Hilary looked at the flowers. She hated to leave them, picked, to go to waste. "I'll give them to my mother," she said.

TWELVE

A Speech at School

Mrs. Toft was surprised to receive the flowers. She said nothing beyond "thank you" when they were given to her, and took them into the kitchen to put them into water. She noticed that amongst them there were some astrantias, a favorite of her mother's not often found in England, and so she knew that they must have some connection with the plants that the two girls had brought back from Lewes. She wondered again whether she ought not to know something more about this mystery; she would have liked to feel really assured that it was all quite right.

At tea she was still pondering on this subject. Hilary was chattering away at her usual rate and David was not condescending to listen to her. He usually considered his sister as quite beneath his notice, and so Mrs. Toft was surprised out of her reverie when suddenly she heard him speak. "Why," he asked, "does Hilary put biscuits in her pocket?" He spoke as if he had been observing the habits of some lower animal and felt constrained to inquire about one of its more puzzling traits.

"Hilary!" said her mother sharply.

But Hilary was already speaking herself.

"It's none of your business, David!" she cried. "Oh, Mummy! I don't feel like eating them now and I've only taken my share. Look!" And she produced the biscuits and laid them on the table.

"No one wants them after they've been in your pocket, Hilary," said Mrs. Toft with distaste. There always seems to be a deposit of dust in the bottom of pockets, and in Hilary's—since she had spent so much time crawling about the garden—there was plenty of earth and fragments of leaves and grass. All this adhered liberally to the surface of the biscuits.

"May I keep them then?" asked Hilary, eagerly.

Mrs. Toft looked at David, who looked very disapproving. This made her laugh, and she said, "Yes, I suppose so."

After tea Hilary heard her mother calling her from the kitchen and she went in great trepidation, expecting to be scolded properly about the biscuits and warned never to do such a thing again. Instead she found her mother rooting in the back of the kitchen cupboard. Presently she emerged, saying, "Now, would this do for your biscuits, Hilary?" and handed her a small round tin that had once held oatcakes.

"Oh, thank you, it would be lovely," she said, taking the tin in surprise.

"And is this connected with the secret, too?" asked Mrs. Toft, suddenly looking Hilary very straight in the eye.

"The secret?" said Hilary, so taken aback that she almost dropped the tin.

"Yes, all these mysterious goings on. The biscuits, the flowers you have just brought me, the plants you brought up from Granny's, and the long hours you spend I don't know where. Aren't they all a secret?"

"Well, yes," admitted Hilary, dreading more.

"And are you sure, Hilary, that it is something I should approve of, if I knew all about it? You're not doing anything wrong, are you?"

"Oh, no, Mummy."

"Are you quite sure? Do think it out, dear. I don't want you running into mischief or doing anything dishonest or wrong."

"Oh, no; we're not doing anything wrong. I'm quite sure, really, Mummy."

"And there's nothing bad connected with it?"

"No, nothing."

"Very well, I won't ask you anything more about it, and I hope I can trust you, Hilary, not to do anything you are in the least bit doubtful about. If you're not sure whether it's right, don't do it. Or ask me."

"Yes, Mummy. I will."

On the whole Hilary was very pleased that her mother had guessed so much of the secret. She lay thinking of it in bed that night and was very happy when she realized that all the subterfuge she had practiced lately in concealing the secret would be no longer necessary. There was nothing wrong in their secret, of course. She remembered how Dickon, in the story of *The Secret Garden* had told his mother of the secret and she had said it was all good and right. And so *their* secret garden was all good and right too.

Then suddenly she remembered Bridget's truant playing. She had forgotten it entirely when she had been talking to her mother. That was wrong, certainly, and so she should have told her of it. What would her mother have said? What would she have done? Hilary could not imagine. And that horrid wicked note that Bridget was to present to Miss Mills tomorrow? If only there was some other way out of it. This was dishonesty and cheating and Hilary writhed when she thought of it. It was something that would make her mother very angry and it made Hilary angry too, but she could think of nothing to do about it. What could one do with a person like Bridget who did things like that?

Anyway, it should not happen again. Hilary was half glad that she had honestly forgotten it when talking with her mother. Of course, she ought to tell her. She would, if Bridget played truant again. But she would see that Bridget did not. She *must* come to school tomorrow. And meanwhile Hilary would speak to those other girls, and put the fear of God into them. None of them should bully Bridget again.

For a long time she could not think of an occasion when she would be able to get the others together without Bridget. And then she remembered when she would have a perfect opportunity. When Bridget arrived in the morning she would have to take her hateful note to the headmistress. That always took a long time; there was usually a long queue of girls with notes waiting outside Miss Mills's room.

During that time all the girls would be in the classroom waiting for their teacher to arrive and call the roll.

The next day Bridget did come to school. Hilary met her in the corridor going down to Miss Mills's room and she hurried up to the classroom while the coast was clear.

Everyone was already there. She noticed that Catherine was standing by her desk chatting with one or two other more virtuous girls. But most of the class, which included all those who usually bullied Bridget, were gathered at the back of the room. Hilary went straight up to them and said:

"You great cads and bullies! You lily-livered cowards! You maggot-ridden lumps of rancid lard! You scabs . . ." She had invented a great many more epithets in bed the night before but her audience would let her get no further with them. Their leader was at her side twisting her arm and all the others had crowded round her in a menacing manner.

"We all know Hilary is so tactful," said one of them with a snigger.

"What have we done?"

"Yes, what have we done?" echoed some others.

"You just take back all that," bawled the one who was twisting her arm.

Hilary, however, was not in the least intimidated. She wrenched her arm free and, folding it with the other across her chest, struck an attitude which suggested that she had great things to tell, and waited until a silence of curiosity had fallen. Even Catherine and her friends had dropped their conversation and were listening.

Then Hilary spoke.

"At the beginning of last term a new girl came into our midst," she said, "and when she entrusted her to us, our august headmistress,"—Hilary had got into her stride as a public speaker by now,—"our august headmistress exhorted us to be kind to her. And who here," she went on, raising her voice in appeal, "who here can honestly look into her heart and say 'I have been kind to this poor motherless orphan'? Which of you has not bullied her, baited her, and made her life a misery? Surely you deserve to be called cads and bullies!"

Some girls laughed at this eloquence, but it was uneasy laughter. Most of them began violently and indignantly to deny the charges.

"I like that! And coming from you, Miss Hilary Toft! We've only tried to talk to her. And who is it has plagued her more than anyone with her talking?"

"We've treated her quite normally. It's her fault if she doesn't like it. We can't help that."

"I'd like to hear anyone else tell us we've been unkind to her. That's your opinion, maybe, but it's not so, is it, Catherine?"

Catherine was still standing by her desk a little way from the group, watching. Several people turned to her and there was a hush to hear her verdict. She was generally respected, and what she said would be taken seriously, though they might mock Hilary.

"Well," she said, falteringly, "you *do* bully her, you know."

Further discussion of the matter was prevented, however, by the entry of their teacher.

Perhaps the fact that none of the girls had an opportunity to talk to one another about what had been said made them think the more about it. Bridget joined the class as they filed into the hall for prayers, and already many of the girls tried to make way for her with special kindness, prompted by their consciences.

Providence had guided the headmistress to choose a lesson and hymn which suggested to them all that they should have taken a more loving care of Bridget. The lesson was the Parable of the Good Samaritan, and the hymn they sang contained the words—

> Help us to help each other, Lord,
> Each other's cross to bear.

So they came out of prayers feeling very pious and with plenty of good intentions formed in their minds. And during the next few days, even weeks, everyone was making a special effort on Bridget's behalf, and treating her with extra consideration. Hilary patted herself on the back and took all the credit for this improvement. Bridget herself must have noticed it, but what she thought about it no one could tell. Anyway, she did not play truant again.

THIRTEEN

Mrs. Sanders Catches a Thief

The weather was very unsettled and for some days seemed to be brewing up for a thunderstorm. Heavy showers alternated with sunny patches and all the time there were grey clouds low in the sky; their color suggested lead and they seemed to be weighing down on the atmosphere, making it close and steamy. Everything in the garden grew apace, but the nettles seemed to outstrip all else. For some time they had shown signs of a revival in the old greenhouse and now they sprang up in such abundance that they almost hid the plants.

Now that Mrs. Toft knew part of the secret, they were able to borrow tools and such things from her openly, which often made the work much easier. Pulling up the nettles was not a job that appealed to Hilary. Gardening enthusiasm came to her occasionally but it never lasted very long, particularly when a job like this presented itself. So Bridget did most of the work.

The seeds that they had planted were beginning to come into flower now. There was the clarkia, which Hilary decided she didn't like. "They're all dingy petticoat colors," she said. She also felt bound to dislike the nasturtiums. "I like flowers that smell nice," she said. But they had grown so profusely and flowered in such a variety of flame colors that she had to admit that they made a brave show. The others she admired less grudgingly. She was forever sticking her nose into the mignonette and drawing in deep breaths with an ecstatic expression of the face, like the children on the Bisto tins. It was on one of these occasions that she made the disparaging remarks about the nasturtiums. But what pleased her most of all was the schizanthus. "I chose that," she said with pride.

Hilary always felt that the flowers belonged to Bridget, although they had both paid for the seeds. "They'd never have grown for me, I'm sure," she said. "Granny would say you've got green fingers. Things grow for you that wouldn't grow for other people." And this was true, for there were the schizanthus plants and the little prim French marigolds flourishing and flowering, while many people cannot grow these unless they start them in a greenhouse. Bridget always stood by in silence when Hilary praised or criticized the flowers, rather as if they were her workmanship.

The briars in the old rose garden were coming out too.

"Do you think that there'll be any real roses amongst them?" asked Hilary.

"No, there won't. The briar's much stronger and chokes the cultivated rose."

"But there might be just one rose left in the midst that hadn't been choked. One last surviving rose."

"Not after all these years. Not unless someone's pruned them since this place was bombed."

"Well, perhaps someone has, just as they did in the story of *The Secret Garden.*"

"You can look for yourself, but I don't think so."

So they went to make a search where the impenetrable thicket of briars was flecked with white and pink of dog roses. The briars had grown so much that spring that it was now almost impossible to force a way round to the summerhouse, but they made themselves a passage. Hilary searched high and low, but in the end she had to admit that Bridget was right: there was not one cultivated rose left.

These days the garden seemed so very much their own that they did not always take the precautions they had taken earlier. One day when they were leaving by the shrubbery they came round a corner and suddenly saw a young man in khaki coming towards them. He had almost surely seen them, but nevertheless they acted on their first instinct and jumped into the bushes. The young soldier came sauntering on. He peered into the bushes where he had seen them disappear and saw them crouching amongst the ivy.

"Good afternoon," he said. It did not seem to strike him as funny.

"Good afternoon," replied Hilary, whom surprise never robbed of her tongue.

The young man sauntered on and when he was out of sight they stood up and got out of the bushes.

"We must have looked silly," said Hilary. Then suddenly she noticed Bridget's face. "What's the matter?" she exclaimed. "You look terrified. Your face is—sort of twitching."

Bridget looked very white and frightened and her face was twitching in a curious way. She put her hand up to cover it.

"Whatever is the matter? What's happened?"

"I can't help it," mumbled Bridget, referring to the twitch. "It happens sometimes when I'm very frightened."

"But what's frightened you? Not that soldier?"

"Yes."

"But why? He hadn't even got a gun to shoot us with!"

"I thought he had. I didn't see," Bridget muttered sullenly.

"But why should he shoot us? In London? And in peacetime?"

"I suppose I'm silly," said Bridget, and then she went silent. Although she said no more, the incident remained in Hilary's memory and she felt there must be some explanation behind Bridget's terror. She wondered if the soldier had reminded her of German soldiers in Guernsey during the War. Perhaps something horrible had happened to her then.

Meanwhile they had started some more work in the garden. This time they had decided to make the summer-house into a pleasant hideout for wet weather. They scrubbed and swept and Hilary found some old tins of paint at home, with which they could touch up the inside.

"Anyone can see someone's been at work here if they explore as far as this," said Hilary as she surveyed her handiwork. "But still, there's no point in coming here if we can't make it nice for ourselves. Anyway, I don't suppose we shall be able to come for long."

"What do you mean by that?" asked Bridget.

"Oh, I daresay they'll be building on this whole site soon. You don't think it'll stay deserted like this forever, do you?"

Bridget remembered that Mrs. Toft had said much the same thing when she had first pointed out the gardens from the bus. But since then she had forgotten it, and had begun to think of their garden as a refuge forever. The reminder gave her a jolt, but all she said was, "I wonder what they will build."

The idea that the garden would not last forever made them want to go there more often. When all the jobs there were done for the moment, they came simply to read or do their homework. If it was fine they could work in their lair under the apple trees or else in the grass on the lawn. For the lawn, which had once been an exposed place they had avoided, was now so deep in hay that it gave them ample cover. If you stood up, the grass tops came well up to the waist, and sitting or lying you were quite hidden. On ground level they had worked themselves a maze of tunnels through which they could crawl unseen or lie looking up at the sky through a mesh of ripening hay. Then, in wet weather, there was the summerhouse or the boiler house, though the latter was not much good for reading because there was no window to let in the light. It was a small room, half below the ground, backing against the greenhouse wall. Inside was the boiler, very quaint and old-fashioned, which obviously had not seen use for many years, even before the bombing, and the bunkers that had once held coal. The whole place was flooded with dead leaves. One stepped in them up to the knees, and in the corners they reached as high as the ceiling, where they were held in place by thick nets of cobwebs. It was here, hidden in the leaves, that Hilary and Bridget kept their tin of biscuits.

As time went on their store of biscuits increased, as they did not eat many of them. It was understood that they were a provision against some unforeseen need. The two of them were not, of course, laying plans for Bridget to play truant again, but it was as well to be provided for anything that might turn up.

Hilary's mother let her have a couple of biscuits from time to time, and Bridget, too, brought her contributions. But Bridget did not get her biscuits in the way Hilary did. When she had said, "We could get them from home," she had meant that she could pilfer them from the tin in her aunt's kitchen cupboard without her aunt's knowledge. It did not enter her head that Hilary might think this was wrong, or that that was not how she got her biscuits too. And nothing had happened to bring this little matter to light.

One evening Bridget went into the back kitchen to get biscuits, as she had done before. Her aunt and cousin were in the front basement room and her uncle was upstairs, so there was no one about. She went to the cupboard and opened it to look for the tin, but inside the cupboard it was too dark to see properly.

"No one will notice if I turn the light on," she thought; "they are all too busy."

So she switched on the light and went to the cupboard again. Now it was easy to see the biscuit tin and she reached it out and was lifting the lid when suddenly behind her a man's voice, loud and resonant, said:

"And now we will take you to our London studio."

At first she was too surprised to realize what had happened. She stood frozen at the cupboard, her hand trembling on the tin and the sweat in beads upon her forehead. She did not dare to turn round. Then as the voice went on she realized what had happened: it was the radio that she had turned on in turning on the light, and it had taken those few seconds to warm up. In a moment she was at the switch and had turned it off. But as she stood in the darkness, which seemed so much darker by contrast with the light, she heard a door open, and her aunt's footsteps in the passage. There was no time for escape. The door opened, her aunt was there and had switched on the light so that the commentator's voice resumed in mid-sentence, only missing a few words.

"Well, what's this?" asked her aunt. "What are you doing here?"

Bridget stood dumbly and dared not sneak a glance at the cupboard door which was open, with the biscuit

tin at the front, its lid half raised. But her aunt had seen it already.

"So I've caught you redhanded, have I? I thought the biscuits were going," she said. There was fury in her voice. "Well, what have you to say for yourself?"

Bridget had nothing to say, but the radio went on talking, oblivious of them. Mrs. Sanders went across and switched it off.

"Well, what have you to say for yourself?"

There was silence in the lighted kitchen.

"Don't I give you enough to eat?"

This was asked in a furious voice and Bridget did not dare to answer Yes or No. The latter would certainly not have been true.

Mrs. Sanders was with difficulty restraining herself from grasping Bridget and shaking her. The silence of the girl infuriated her. She stood a yard away from her, all tense with anger.

"Well, don't I give you enough to eat? I should think I do. You ought to be grateful for it. You've known hunger during the war, in Guernsey. Do you think it's easy, feeding a growing child when everything's still rationed? But have I ever grudged you food?"

Bridget's eyes were on the floor and she said nothing.

"There! You can't deny it. And you'd better not either, for I don't know who'd feed you if I didn't. You've tried the patience of all your other relations."

At this point Mrs. Sanders went to the cupboard, rammed down the lid of the tin and slammed the cupboard door. Perhaps she felt the need for exercise. Bridget thought that the moment had come for her to depart, but her aunt saw her movement and barked out, "Don't you go thinking that you can get off yet! I haven't had my say out, and you've to apologize. Stand where you are."

She walked over to Bridget and went on. "So you steal things out of my cupboard, do you, you little thief?" She put a bitter emphasis on the words "steal" and "thief." "Here am I, toiling and moiling to get enough food to go round, and you steal it out of my cupboard. And biscuits are rationed. I know you know that. Is little Robin to go without because you can't keep your hands from picking and stealing? I asked your uncle, when he said we'd have to take you in, had he thought what it would be having another mouth to feed with rationing and all? But I never thought it would come to this, with you *stealing* food. And do you think I want a thief in this house, with my little Robin? Your uncle may say you've got nowhere else to go, but he's got his own child's welfare to think of."

Mrs. Sanders made a pause at this point to let what she had said sink in. Never before in the scenes she had made had she threatened to turn Bridget out of the house. Now she felt rather horrified with herself. It was something she had always prevented herself from saying and now she had said it. She felt ashamed of herself, but shame is not a very pleasant thing, and feeling it did not improve Mrs. Sanders' temper.

"Well, what are you standing there whimpering for?"

she snapped. "You're not out on the streets, not this time. But don't let it happen again. Are you sorry?"

Bridget uttered a scarcely audible, "Yes."

"Go on, say it properly!"

"I am very sorry."

"And I should hope you are. And you can go straight to bed now,"—which Bridget did, with the utmost speed.

FOURTEEN

Bridget's Story

After school the next day the two of them went up to the garden. Hilary had two biscuits to put in the tin. Bridget, of course, had none. They did not intend spending any time in the garden that evening and as they came out of the boiler house Hilary turned to go to the gap in the wall.

"Let's go to our lair," proposed Bridget.

"If you like," said Hilary, although she wanted to get back to her tea.

Bridget led the way, and when they reached the lair she sat down on the ground. Hilary remained standing, for tea was still uppermost in her mind.

"What do you want to do?" she asked, hoping it would not take long.

Bridget plucked a long weed stalk and did not answer for a moment. Then she said, in a curious stubborn way, "I don't want to go home."

"What do you mean?"

"I don't want to go home."

"Well," said Hilary, puzzled, "I daresay you could come to tea with us." Anything, so long as she could get back to tea quickly.

"I mean I don't want to go back to my aunt's, ever."

"Whatever's happened?" Hilary stood with her mouth hanging open. All thoughts of tea had fled. Then she sat down. "Tell me."

Bridget picked a long spray of willow herb and began to pull the leaves to pieces, beginning at the top. Her hands and eyes thus occupied, she told her tale.

When Hilary heard how she had been taking the biscuits without her aunt's knowledge or permission, she was very shocked.

"You shouldn't have done that. You know you shouldn't. Why, it's as good as stealing."

It had not entered Bridget's head that Hilary would disapprove. It made her story seem rather flat and so she did not want to go on with it. Probably she would get no sympathy. She became very sullen and gave all her attention to her operations on the willow herb.

"Well, go on," urged Hilary. "What happened next?"

"You don't want to hear."

"Yes. I do."

"I don't want to tell you if you think I am a thief."

"I didn't say you were a thief. I only said it was very wrong to take the biscuits. I don't think you're a thief, really I don't. Do tell me what happened next."

So Bridget, mollified, went on to explain how the radio

worked in the kitchen and how it had brought her aunt in.

"And she was furious. She said she didn't want me in the house any longer. She said I was a bad influence on Robin. And that there wasn't enough food to go round, anyway. But I don't eat much," she added, her voice breaking into sobs.

"Oh, she didn't mean that! Don't cry. She only lost her temper. You mustn't take it seriously. She didn't mean it."

Bridget choked for a little while and then she swallowed her sobs and said, "I'm not going back there, anyway. They don't want me. They only took me in because they felt they had to. I'm never going back there."

"Don't be silly. You must. It's not true, what you think, I'm sure. People say things in tempers that they don't mean. Cheer up." Then Hilary had a happy inspiration. "Come home to tea," she said, "and talk it over with my mother."

Bridget gulped. "She'd say I was a thief," she muttered.

"No, she wouldn't. She'd think it was very wrong to take the biscuits like that, maybe, but she'd understand. You know she would."

Bridget wept on, a little more freely and naturally now that she saw some hope of real sympathy in sight.

"Come on," said Hilary, thinking of tea once more. Then she laughed suddenly, thinking of the funny side of the situation. "What was it the radio said? Tell me again."

" 'Now we will take you to our London studio'."

Bridget's face brightened for a moment as she, too, saw the funny side.

"Wasn't it odd to catch it just when it was saying that? What a fright to give you! You must have thought it was the Gestapo come to fetch you, or something."

At Hilary's words a different look came over Bridget's face. Her eyes seemed to be looking into the far, far distance, or perhaps into the past. Her mouth was slightly open and her hands employed themselves mechanically on the remains of the willow herb.

"What have I said now?" asked Hilary. She had risen for departure.

Bridget's eyes still had their far-off look and her voice sounded far off too as she said, "I did live in Guernsey in the War, when the Germans were there. I told you a lie before."

Hilary sat down, tea forgotten. Now she would get to the bottom of the mystery. "And did the Germans—the Gestapo come after you?" she asked.

"No, they never came for me."

"Please, tell me all about it. Did you live with your parents? What was it like with the Germans there?"

"My father was dead," Bridget began; "he was a soldier and was killed in action at the beginning of the War. I was living with my mother when the Germans came."

She paused. Even now that she had decided to tell her story she found it difficult. Words did not come easily. Her voice sounded strange to herself and she was shy. Hilary waited while she paused, and then she prompted her to go on by asking a question.

"Was it in the town or country that you lived?"

"Oh, in the country. In a house all by itself on the top of a little hill."

"Of course, you grew grapes there. I forgot."

"Oh, we didn't grow grapes there—that was at the farm. There was a farm a little way off, down the hill. It belonged to us and it was let to some people called Champignon. As you know, a lot of people in Guernsey speak French and have French names. These were called Champignon."

"Mushrooms?"

"Yes. Mummy used to call them the Mushrooms."

Another pause. So Hilary prompted again.

"Were they nice, these Champignons?"

"Well, I didn't know them much then. We lived alone up at our house, Mummy and I, and we didn't go out to see the neighbors or anything. But I had to go to live with the Champignons afterwards."

"Afterwards? After what?" Here Hilary knew they were at the core of the matter.

Bridget's eyes gazed into the far, far distance and she was silent some moments. And then she resumed.

"We lived alone together, my mother and I. She used to give me lessons and we did everything together. Sometimes the Germans would come about something and then we were both very frightened. They would come to search the house sometimes, and it was terrifying. I didn't know what they were looking for and whether they would find it."

"Late one evening, after it was dark, they came and

knocked on the door. I was in bed, but I ran downstairs to my mother because I didn't like to be alone upstairs while they were in the house. And this time they found what they were looking for and they took my mother away."

"What was it they were looking for?"

"A radio. We had a radio for hearing the news from England, and it was forbidden."

"Did they let your mother say good-bye?"

"Yes, she kissed me and told me not to be frightened. Then they took her away."

Bridget faltered again, and Hilary prompted her. "What happened next?"

"The next day I waited for my mother to come back. I sat at the window to watch for her, but she did not come, all day. Towards evening I saw Mrs. Champignon coming up the hill, and she came to the gate and called up to me. So I went to the door and asked her to come in, but she wouldn't even come into the garden."

"Why not?"

"She was afraid. She asked me if I had been alone all day and had I had anything to eat. I said, yes, but I had finished everything that was in the larder. And she said that I must come down to the farm, for it wasn't safe for me to be alone at night, and she would give me supper. And I said, suppose my mother came back? And she said she was sure to call at the farm because she would know that they, the Champignons, would be looking after me. So she sent me in to fetch my night things."

"And did your mother come back?"

"No, she didn't come back. And I went on living at the farm from day to day, expecting her, and getting more and more worried, until they had to tell me that she was dead."

A hush descended on the garden. Bridget sat gazing into nothingness, rolling and unrolling the long leaves of willow herb with fumbling fingers, and the tears ran down her cheeks. Even the tactless Hilary did not dare to prompt at this point. The grief frightened her and awed her and she did not know what to do or say. But presently Bridget continued.

"When I knew she'd never come back, I went up to our house and took out all our favorite things, our books and clothes, and I burnt them."

"But why?"

"Because she was dead."

It did not seem an adequate reason to Hilary for such a waste of good things but she subsided into silence all the same.

"The Germans saw the fire and perhaps they thought it was a signal or something. Anyway I saw them coming up the hill to investigate so I slipped away over the fields and hid. I didn't dare go back to the Champignons' house because the Germans would know I was there, and they might make the Champignons hand me over. So I hid in the farm buildings. There was no point in trying to go very far, because Guernsey is so small. And nobody thought of looking for me almost on the Champignon doorstep."

"But how long was it before you were found?"

"A fortnight or so."

"But what did you eat?"

"Oh, it was late summer and there was lots of fruit about. And tomatoes, too. They grow them by the thousand for the market. And sometimes at night I could slip into the kitchen or dairy and get some bread or milk." And seeing the look of disapproval on Hilary's face she added sarcastically, "I suppose *you* would have starved."

"No fear," ejaculated Hilary, the thought of tea passing through her mind.

"I lived mostly in the cowsheds and the hayloft, actually, until they found me."

"Who found you? The Germans?"

"No, the farm people. It was horrible. I didn't want to stay with the Champignons, but I had to, at first."

"But why? What was wrong with them? Why didn't you want to live with them?"

"I don't know, I can't explain," said Bridget wildly. "I couldn't live *there.* Later they let me live with some other people a little way off, because I kept running away. But the War was almost over then."

Hilary interrupted with a "But I don't see why . . . ?" But Bridget hastily continued, "And when the War was over, as soon as the Germans had left, I was sent to England, to my aunt's."

"The aunt in Surrey?"

"No, I went to my aunt's in Oxford first."

"How many aunts have you lived with?" asked Hilary in surprise. She imagined that perhaps Bridget went to live with each for a year in turn, to distribute the weight of her upkeep.

"Only three. I went to my aunt's in Oxford first, but

she didn't really want me. She hadn't any children and she didn't particularly want one about the house."

"So she passed you on to another aunt?"

"I ran away."

"Oh!" Hilary was taken aback. "And how did you do that?"

"I used to come home from school by bus, so one day I took a bus in the other direction."

"But you were found?"

"They sent the police after me."

"How horrid! That was a nasty thing to do. And when they found you, they sent you to your aunt's in Surrey?"

"Yes."

"And had she any children?"

"Too many. They had a big family. I didn't fit it."

Hilary could well imagine the shy and silent Bridget evading all her hosts' kindly attempts to draw her into the family circle. Soon they would have given up the attempt in exasperation and she would have lived as if she was all by herself, hardly there at all.

"So I ran away."

"Again! And then you came here?"

"Yes. But I'm not going back to my Aunt Sanders."

"And have you any other relations?"

"I don't think so."

So there it was. Hilary realized that Bridget fully intended to do what she said, to run away again. But what was to become of her? Hilary lay silent on her stomach, head in hands, thinking. After a while she asked, "Would you like to come and live with us?"

"Your mother wouldn't want me."

"Of course she would. I'll persuade her."

Bridget looked the other way. She was employed upon another spray of willow herb by now and she gave it her full attention to conceal her feelings. She would very much have liked to live with Mrs. Toft but, "It isn't possible," she thought to herself.

"Would you like to?" persisted Hilary.

"Yes," muttered Bridget, "but she won't want me."

"We'll see about that. Will you go back to your aunt's until it's arranged? It won't be long, I tell you. But we don't want to have to send the police out after you."

"You wouldn't do that, would you?" exclaimed Bridget.

"Of course not. You can trust me, can't you? But all the same you'll go home now, won't you?"

"Very well," muttered Bridget grudgingly.

"I'll see you home," said Hilary rising to her feet. "And I'll see what mood your aunt's in."

Mrs. Sanders turned out to be in a very good mood. She came out into the area smiling when she saw them up above on the pavement. She did not scold Bridget for being so late back from school but told her in tones of utmost kindness that her tea was waiting for her. The kindness, in fact, was rather overdone. She was sorry for many of the things she had said the day before and was now ready to fuss over Bridget.

To Hilary all appeared satisfactory, and she went home hopefully to tea.

FIFTEEN

"Couldn't she come to live with us?"

Hilary sat down to the tea that her mother had left out for her and ate it with a hearty appetite. It was only when she had sufficiently assuaged the pangs of hunger that she began to consider seriously how she should tackle the task she had set herself. How should she approach her mother? Now as she thought it over she began to wonder whether her mother would indeed welcome Bridget into the household. One never knew what grown-ups would think.

Presently her mother came and asked if she had had enough to eat. Then she sat down by the table and said, "Really, Hilary, I wish you would come straight home after school unless you have told me to expect you later. I don't mind at all if I know you are not coming in until late, but today, for instance, you said nothing—and I get very worried sometimes."

"I'm very sorry, Mummy. I meant to come home straight after school today but Bridget kept me talking."

Her mother was shaken with gales of laughter at this explanation. "Oh, Hilary!" she said. "Poor little Bridget *kept* you talking! And who, may I ask, did the talking?"

"You may not think it, but she did. And, Mummy," —Hilary now felt that a suitable moment had arrived— "couldn't she come to live with us?"

"Hilary," replied her mother, "you do suggest the most ridiculous things. Whatever made you think of this?"

"Well, you know all about her, don't you? Mrs. Sanders has told you. And she's not happy there, you know." Hilary wondered how much she should tell of the biscuit-stealing.

"You have a very vivid imagination, my dear. I don't think there is any evidence that Bridget is unhappy at her aunt's."

"Well, she's run away from two aunts before, and she says she is going to run away from this one."

"Ah, she's told you about her former escapades? But the situations were very different then. Naturally she was very unsettled at first when she came away from Guernsey. And to live with a pernickety maiden aunt, the one in Oxford, who didn't like children, was very difficult for a lonely child. But it's different now."

"What about the aunt in Surrey, Mummy?"

"Yes, well, I'm not surprised that she didn't settle down in a family of six boisterous children. After all she'd been an only child, and had not even been to school with other children before she came to England."

"I wonder if the Champignons had any children."

"The who?"

"The people she lived with in Guernsey after her mother was killed."

"I don't know. What has that got to do with it?"

"Nothing. What were we talking about? But, oh,

Mummy, she says she is going to run away from her Aunt Sanders!"

"You're making it into a melodrama, Hilary. I'm sure she will do nothing of the sort. You have too active an imagination."

Mrs. Toft had only seen Bridget in her own house where, of all places except the secret garden, she was most at ease. She had heard her story from Mrs. Sanders and had watched her, as she thought, settle down to ordinary life. Hilary's new version of the matter came as a surprise to her, and she was inclined to give all the credit for it to Hilary's imagination.

"But she said it. Seriously, she said it, Mummy. I mean she said it seriously. She means it."

"Now sit down, Hilary, and consider. Where would she go? One can't just hide in London. What other relation could she expect to be sent to? She hasn't any others. It is all very well running away twice, but there comes a time when one must settle down, and Bridget realizes this, I am sure."

"She could come to us, and then she'd settle down. Oh, she would, Mummy, and I'm sure she'll settle down nowhere else. Really I am!"

"My dear Hilary, you are making mountains out of molehills. Wait and see. Then you'll know that Bridget has no intention of running away."

Thus Mrs. Toft closed the subject and Hilary was left to clear the tea things away and consider a new plan of action. "I should have told Mummy in the first place of her playing truant," she thought to herself. "Then she would not think she was so happy and settled down. I must tell her that now. She'll have to believe me. And what about the stealing? She'll have to know it all, but she won't like it. It's the only way, though."

She began to regret now that she had not brought Bridget home with her as she had first suggested. Bridget in the flesh could not have failed to convince her mother that something was wrong. "Yet," she thought then, "her aunt was very kind when I took her back. Perhaps it *will* all blow over as Mummy says.

"We'll see," she thought, "and I can ask her to tea and then Mummy will see for herself."

Meanwhile Mrs. Toft was also considering what had passed. "Can there be any truth in it?" she wondered. It suddenly seemed odd to her that Bridget should have confided her story to Hilary—she was not the confiding sort nor was Hilary the sort one readily confides in. Under what stress of circumstances would she have been driven to it? Could there be something serious here?

"I must see Bridget for myself," she thought. So that when Hilary asked that Bridget should be invited to tea Mrs. Toft readily consented.

"And, Mummy," said Hilary, trying a new approach, "if she *were* unhappy at her aunt's you *would* let her come and live here, wouldn't you? She'd be happy here, and we'd be very pleased to have her, wouldn't we?"

"Let's cross our bridges when we get to them, Hilary. It's all very well your saying how nice it would be to have her here but none of the responsibility would fall on you."

"What responsibility, Mummy? She would not be any

trouble. If I went to school with her every day she couldn't play truant as she has done. Yes, she played truant, Mummy. That shows she's unhappy, doesn't it?"

"Unhappy at school, perhaps, but not at home. But you see what I mean about responsibility. It is a responsibility to look after any child, but one who runs away and plays truant would be a very great responsibility indeed. Suppose she did run away, what do you think I'd feel like?"

"Oh, but she wouldn't run away, Mummy, not from us."

"That's what you think. But I shouldn't like to take the risk."

Although she finished on this decided note, Mrs. Toft continued to think and worry about it all evening. "I must see Bridget for myself," she said; "and if there is anything at the bottom of it, something will have to be done. That child can't be shuttled to and fro from one aunt to another all her life."

Meanwhile Mrs. Sanders was being as kind as she could to Bridget. The smiling welcome which Hilary had seen her give to Bridget was the result of remorse. As soon as Mrs. Sanders had had time to reflect she regretted many of the things she had said. When Bridget was not there with her irritating way of being so unresponsive and keeping herself to her silent self, Mrs. Sanders remembered how kind she had intended to be to this little homeless niece of her husband's. "I went too far last night," she said to herself. "I didn't mean to make her think that we would turn her out of the house."

After Hilary had gone, Mrs. Sanders sat Bridget down to tea and hovered around her asking, would she have this, or some more of that.

"You must eat as much as you like," she said. "You mustn't think that I really meant what I said about its being difficult to provide for you. In fact, you've such a small appetite that you don't even eat your own rations. If you want anything, do ask for it. Would you like some biscuits now?" And she laid her hand very lovingly on Bridget's arm.

Bridget disliked being touched. She was repelled by her aunt's ostentatious affection. She could only think it insincere after yesterday, and she could not return it. She drew her arm away and muttered, "I don't want any biscuits. I'm sorry I took them."

"You can have as many biscuits as you want," went on Mrs. Sanders, contriving to keep her voice kindly, "only don't take them out of the cupboard without asking me." She felt that she had apologized adequately for all she had said the night before, and, that being all over and done with, things might be expected to run smoothly. But bitter words cannot easily be unsaid. They remain said forever, and if they were intended to hurt, they continue to hurt, despite all apologies. So that all Bridget, left sitting at the tea table, could think was, "She doesn't want me. I'm only a nuisance to her. She's obliged to have me because I'm my uncle's niece, but she'd much rather be rid of me."

Then she began to think of Hilary's suggestion and immediately she thought, "Mrs. Toft won't want me. Why should she? Nobody wants me." And the more she thought of that the more she was sure of it. She began to feel angry that she had told Hilary her story and very angry with herself that she had accepted her suggestion that she should approach her mother. How mortifying it would be when Mrs. Toft said, "No, of course we can't have Bridget to live with us! What a thing to suggest!" Bridget felt herself curling up inside at the thought of it, and her pride rose up and said, "You'll not ask favors of strangers. Your relatives are bound to look after you and you'll have to put up with that." Every time she thought it over she saw Mrs. Toft turning her away from the door. To stay where she was would be better than risking that.

Meanwhile, though Mrs. Toft had given her no indication of the line her thoughts had taken, Hilary was sanguine as to the outcome of the tea party. She felt no twinge of conscience when she told Bridget the next day that her mother was "thinking about it, and wanted to see her." She did not know how close to the truth this was. Bridget, however, was suspicious. She sensed that Hilary had not been told to say anything of the sort, and had invented it to encourage her.

"I don't think she wants me," she said, sullenly. "I don't want to force myself on her. I'd rather not come."

This was not the reception Hilary had expected and it took her aback. "I thought you would have liked to come and live with us," she said.

"Not if your mother doesn't want me. I may as well stay with my own relations."

"But you'll come to tea, won't you?"

"I'd rather not."

Hilary frowned and felt like stamping her foot. "I don't see why not. You've come to tea before. Are you going to stop coming to tea altogether?"

"No, I don't mean that."

"Then come to tea tomorrow, won't you?"

"Very well, if you like," assented Bridget wearily.

And Hilary said she did like, and it was fixed. "So she's not going to run away from her aunt's," she thought. "Mummy's right as usual and I suppose it's for the best." But she could not help feeling a twinge of disappointment that they were not to live together.

SIXTEEN

Words in Anger

The tea party, to Hilary, seemed an abject failure. Bridget was sullen and silent. She refused to talk and avoided even looking at Mrs. Toft. She ate very little tea and spent a great deal of time playing with her food so that her eyes hardly left her plate. If she was spoken to, her reply was muttered and scarcely audible. Her old habit, of being startled by a direct question, had returned to her. "There, she draws her horns in like a little snail," thought Hilary.

After tea she drew her aside. "Why don't you talk to my mother?" she asked.

Bridget gave no reply. She was making an elaborate examination of a blemish in the paintwork.

"Well?" insisted Hilary.

"I'd better go home. I'm not wanted here."

"Nonsense! Whatever has put that into your head?"

Bridget dragged her feet slowly towards the front door. "It's true," she said.

"Where are you going now?" said Hilary, following her down the hall.

"Home." And she took her school beret off the peg.

"Mummy, Mummy, Bridget's going already!" cried out Hilary. "Tell her she must stay!"

Mrs. Toft came out into the hall. "What, are you going already, Bridget? Won't you stay any longer?"

"I'd better go," said Bridget, looking in another direction.

"What a pity! But you know you're always welcome here, my dear. Treat it as your own home. Don't wait for Hilary to ask you. I'm always glad to see you."

Bridget looked up momentarily into Mrs. Toft's face and then she put on her beret and went.

"I don't know what's come over her," said Hilary, and she wished that Bridget had talked more and opened her heart to her mother. But really Mrs. Toft was more impressed by Bridget's return to shyness and silence than she would have been by her chattering or confiding. "There is something wrong here," she thought. "I must get to the bottom of it."

Hilary and Bridget still went to the garden these days, and spent much of the weekends there. It was June and the weather was settled and fine and it was lovely to be there, out of doors. The briars were still patched with white and pink and the willow herb had broken out into a deeper pink; there were seas of it, pink seas shifting gently in the wind. The wind also brought the heavy scent of syringa from the bushes in the shrubbery which were white with blossom. The lime trees were in flower, and the smell filled the garden.

Hilary would have liked to spend her time lying on her back looking up at the blue sky and inhaling the different scents as the wind drifted them over her nose. But Bridget was driven by an insane energy. She could never be still, she must always be doing something strenuous. She worked hard at the garden and Hilary felt constrained to help her, though usually she tired of it quickly and went off to take a rest. Bridget never tired of it. Or if she did, she went on working all the same, finding some pleasure in making her limbs ache and her hands sore. When all the usual work on their own patches of garden was done, she found more work for herself. She started to strip the bindweed that had matted over various bushes under the apple trees. Unveiled, they turned out to be gooseberry bushes and currants. Hilary came and ate the gooseberries, but they were small and sour. Then Bridget turned to completely pointless jobs. She cleared weeds and nettles where they had no intention of planting anything.

"What are you doing that for?" asked Hilary.

Bridget turned and looked at her, but she said nothing. Then she went on with her work. So Hilary shook her head and went and lay down in the hay. But she was worried about Bridget. What had come over her? In the garden she used to be so open and happy. Now she was as silent and sullen there as anywhere else and always this work, work, work. She used to lead the way. Now she went by herself, and Hilary felt that Bridget almost resented it when she went to work by her side.

Yes, she was worried about Bridget. Did she intend to

run away from her aunt's? Hilary imagined her disappearing into the great whirling metropolis of London and never being seen again. This must not happen. Hilary would prevent it. Nearly every day she walked all the way to Banbury Terrace with her, ignoring hints that she was not wanted, even if she perceived them. And she was not contented to leave Bridget until she had seen her safely down the area steps into her aunt's keeping.

Things were not running as smoothly in the Sanders household as Mrs. Sanders had hoped they would. Bridget did not respond at all to the new kindly treatment. She was herself too miserable and too much in need of understanding to realize that her aunt needed a little understanding and help too. She only knew that the kindness was not heartfelt and that it was a poor substitute for ordinary affection. Meanwhile the constant effort to be kind was a great strain on Mrs. Sanders. "Here I am," she complained to her husband, "exerting myself to the utmost to be loving to this unlovable child, and she doesn't even seem to notice it. I can't bear living with anyone so secretive!"

Mr. Sanders did not think that either of his sisters would be willing to take Bridget back, but he suggested that she might be sent to boarding school if his wife really wished it. But Mrs. Sanders thought it would be a pity to move Bridget from a school where she had actually found herself a friend.

Tea time was the worst ordeal because Mr. Sanders was not there so Mrs. Sanders had no one to talk to. "If only Bridget would pull herself together and try to talk to me, then we could be friends," she thought one evening. Out loud she asked, "What have you been doing at school today?" But irritation showed in her voice.

Bridget flinched. "Nothing much," she murmured.

"What lessons did you have?" Mrs. Sanders asked, with forced patience.

"French, math, gym, and art, English and history," Bridget recited this timetable slowly, but without any expression in her voice.

"Which is your favorite?"

Bridget bit her lip and said, "I dunno."

Her aunt could no longer conceal her exasperation. "Well," she snapped, "if you don't deign to talk to me, you had better leave the table. Go up to your own room where you've no one but yourself to talk to."

Almost every other night there was some sort of scene at the tea table, although it did not always end with Bridget's being sent to bed. But sometimes Mrs. Sanders did lose her temper and sent Bridget to her room, and then afterwards she would be sorry, and she would go upstairs to fetch Bridget and speak kindly to her.

One day when Bridget had come home from school little Robin chose to ask her a question at tea.

"Did you have lunch at school, B'idget?" he asked.

"Yes," she replied, startled.

"Is it a nice lunch?"

"All right."

"What did you have today, B'idget?"

"I've forgotten."

"What do you mean, you've forgotten?"

She gave no reply to this.

"Tell me what you had for lunch today," Robin insisted.

Bridget ate in silence.

"Go on, tell me, do!"

Mrs. Sanders had been reading the evening paper. She looked over the top and snapped, "Answer your cousin."

"I've forgotten," muttered Bridget.

Her aunt threw down the paper. "Are we all to sit in silence because you are here? Is there to be no civilized conversation while you are in the room? Are you to snap at little Robin because he asks you an innocent question? Let me tell you that if you're going to go on living in this house you've got to behave like a normal human being."

Bridget was silently crying.

"We are normal happy people and if you can't join in with us you shall be sent to boarding school, and you'll see how you like that. I'll speak to your uncle tonight."

SEVENTEEN

Runaway

It was Friday night, and Hilary was in her bath when she heard the telephone ring. She heard the drawing room door open and her mother's footsteps go across the hall and the ringing stop abruptly at half-gasp. But she was much more interested in blowing soap bubbles than in the telephone and she had quite forgotten about it when a minute later her mother called out, "Are you out of your bath yet, Hilary?"

"Yes, Mummy," she replied, leaping out in the same moment to make her words true.

"Then come down here a moment, dear," called up her mother.

Hilary came bounding downstairs barefoot and wet under her dressing gown, and found her mother saying Yes and No at irregular intervals into the telephone. So she stood by and waited with no idea of what was up.

"Yes. . . . Well, yes. . . . I don't know. . . . Hilary said something about it. . . . Yes, apparently she'd mentioned it to Hilary. . . . Well, here is Hilary. Perhaps you'd like to speak to her yourself."

The truth dawned upon Hilary just as her mother put her hand over the mouthpiece to explain the situation to her. "It's Mrs. Sanders. Bridget hasn't come home tonight. Will you speak to her?"

Hilary took the receiver. "Hullo."

"Is that you, Hilary?"

"Yes, it's me."

"When did you last see Bridget?"

"Let me see. After school today I left her on the corner of Ladbroke Terrace and that other road that Banbury Terrace turns out of. I didn't go quite all the way home with her."

"This was immediately after school?"

"Yes, we came straight back."

"And she said something about running away?"

"Not today. No."

"But she seemed queer or upset?"

"Not specially. Much the same as she has this last fortnight."

"Oh, has she been behaving oddly this last fortnight?"

"Well, yes. It's since she said she would run away. But I thought she'd decided not to."

"Well, she has. And, Hilary, we are relying on you to help us find her. You must have some idea where she would go."

Hilary paused.

"I don't know where she is," she said.

Mrs. Sanders sounded very irritated on the other end of the phone. "This is no time for childish games," she said. "Bridget is very naughty to run away, and it's your duty to tell me where she is."

"But I don't know where she is."

"Don't you realize that this is serious? You can't behave like a baby in circumstances like this. What good can you do Bridget by concealing her?"

"I've told you! I don't know where she is!"

"Naughty girl! May I speak to your mother again?"

Hilary handed the receiver to her mother and sat down on the foot of the stairs. A long conversation ensued. ". . . Well if you like . . . if you think it's really necessary . . . yes . . . yes . . . no, I don't think so . . . ," and so on, until at last Mrs. Toft put down the receiver and said, "Well, she insists on coming round here. Why haven't you got your pajamas on?"

"I'd only just got out of the bath."

"Well go and put then on. Wait a minute—"

"Yes?"

"You've not got Bridget hidden in your room or anything have you?"

"Oh, no, Mummy!"

"Did you know she was going to run away today?"

"No. I'd have seen her right home if I'd known, I've done that before, you know."

"Have you? Well, Mrs. Sanders is calling out the police to look for Bridget."

"But Bridget's not a criminal! Why should the police be sent after her?"

"Of course she's not a criminal, but she must be found, and Mrs. Sanders can't do that all by herself. I know it's not pleasant to call in the police, but we have to. Go up and put your pajamas on."

Mrs. Sanders arrived with a policeman. Mr. Sanders had stayed behind because little Robin could not be left alone in the house. She was getting hysterical and wept a lot, and shouted at Hilary. But the policeman was very polite and said he hoped the little girl would be able to help them to find her little friend, and had she any idea where she might be?

Hilary had felt rather guilty about concealing her knowledge from Mrs. Sanders. Was it really the right thing to do? But she had no qualms about misleading the police. She did not want to tell them lies, but otherwise she would do her best to prevent them finding Bridget. So she thought for a long time and then she said, "Well, I don't know."

"Never mind if you think it sounds ridiculous," said the policeman. "Any information you can give may be very useful to us."

"Ah well," said Hilary, "she never told me where she would hide when she ran away."

"But there must have been some place where you went often that would suggest itself to her. Did you go to Kensington Gardens often, for instance?"

"We went there sometimes." They had been there twice.

"Or any other place you can think of?"

"I remember she told me that when she ran away before she took a bus into the country."

"Ah yes, I believe that Mrs. Sanders here has told us that. It is a possibility." And he noted it down in a note book. "And is that all you can tell us?"

"Yes," said Hilary. Yes, that was all she could tell them. She was in honor bound not to give their secret garden away. All the time she knew that her mother's eyes were upon her, but she did not dare look at her. She dreaded that she might interrupt, and consider it her grown-up duty to give what she knew away and make Hilary tell the rest. But Mrs. Toft did not.

Presently the policeman excused himself and went away to conduct the search, but Mrs. Sanders stayed. She was weeping copiously, and bemoaning alternately her lot and Bridget's.

"Poor child, poor child," she cried. "But we did our best for her. Now she has nowhere to go and I don't know what will become of her.

"But oh dear! It has been a trial having her in the house! You'll not believe it, Mrs. Toft, but she never speaks a word. Not a word! It was becoming more than I could stand. I was very sorry for her, of course, but she wasn't quite honest. She used to steal things, and I'm sure she told lies. She was so secretive, it wasn't quite natural.

"She'll have to go to some institution now, where perhaps they'll look after her better than an ordinary family could, and find out what's wrong with her. I could never let her come in my house again. My husband agrees that it would be better for her to be sent somewhere else. It has been too much for me. I'd not be surprised if I was taken ill after all this, it's been such a strain."

Hilary's father had retired into the dining room to work, leaving his wife to deal with the hysterical woman, but Hilary sat watching and listening until her mother told her to go to bed. Still Mrs. Sanders stayed on. Hilary in her room above could hear endless laments and recriminations murmuring through the floor.

"Is she going to stay here all night?" Hilary asked herself. She was sitting up in bed hugging her knees, because every time she lay down she almost dropped off to sleep. It was essential that she should keep awake because she had formed the plan to go and look for Bridget herself. At first she had been very doubtful that Bridget would have hidden in the garden; it was so obvious. But then, after all, it was only obvious to her, Hilary, and Bridget might trust her. Yes, the more she thought about it, the more sure she became that the garden would be Bridget's hideout—there were the biscuits there, and their own elaborately contrived hiding places. So long as Hilary did not give it away, it was the best place in London to hide.

"When *is* she going to go?" thought Hilary. Mrs. Sanders's voice could still be heard wailing and bemoaning downstairs. Until she had left, and her parents had gone to bed, Hilary could not leave the house. She thought of Bridget alone in the garden and she longed to go and join her, and persuade her to come home and throw herself on Mrs. Toft's mercy. "Surely Mummy will take her in then," she thought. She was reckoning without Bridget's pride.

How difficult it was to keep awake! She stood up on her bed and opened the big sash window over it and sat out on the window sill. There were ridges that stuck into her, but that was all to the good because it kept her awake; and the fresh air in her face also helped. It was one of those very long days just after midsummer and the clear sky was still light with the departed sun. A large moon had risen and it was difficult to tell whether there was more light coming from the sky or from the moon. The light was very soft and diffused and white, but as Hilary sat watching it, trying to decide which source it came from, the shadows darkened and the light grew sharper and colder. The day had faded at last from the sky, and a pure metallic moonlight was left.

Downstairs Hilary heard the drawing room door open. At last Mrs. Sanders was going. There was talk in the hall, and then the front door slammed and Mrs. Toft's footsteps came back across the hall. Hilary heard her talking to the cat. "Now she will come up to bed and so will Daddy," she thought.

But, no. They were going into the drawing room. They were talking. There was a little mew outside the door. Hilary went and let Pip into her room. He curled up next to her on the bed and she stroked him softly while she listened to the rise and fall of voices from below.

What did they want to sit up and talk so late for? It was mostly her father's voice she heard and he talked a lot, as he usually did, for Hilary took after him. There would be gaps when she could just discern her mother's quieter voice, and then her father would come in again. But although his voice was loud, the ceiling and floor between muffled the words and only an occasional one came through. An odd word meant little and conveyed nothing to Hilary. She shifted her legs from under the cat, for he was very heavy, and was giving her pins and needles. He was only too pleased to have the opportunity to occupy a central position on the bed leaving only just enough room for Hilary to sit with her feet tucked under her.

There was her father's voice again. She could hear the words that time. What was it he had said? "It would be a great responsibility to undertake." What was that? A great responsibility to undertake. . . .

Oh dear! She had fallen asleep. "Pip, move over!" she whispered rubbing her eyes. Ah! there were doors opening and closing downstairs. That was what had awakened her. They would be going up to bed at last. Then she could go out. She mustn't go to sleep again.

Yes, they were coming upstairs. There were her mother's footsteps on the linoleum of the upper landing. "Why, she's coming to my door!" Hilary quickly dug her legs down underneath the cat.

The door opened, and Mrs. Toft came into the dark room. "Are you awake?" she asked, softly. "Ah, you've got the cat there."

Hilary sat up in bed.

"Put your clothes on, dear. We must go out and look for Bridget."

EIGHTEEN

Expedition by Moonlight

Hilary was so surprised that she obeyed without asking any questions. When she was almost dressed her mother said, "I suppose you *do* know where she will be."

"I don't *know* she'll be there."

"We shall need a flashlight, I suppose?"

"Yes. I've never been there at night before."

"I should hope not. Do up your shoes. There is no need to leave the laces dangling like that."

They went downstairs and Mr. Toft fetched them a large powerful flashlight. "I don't like letting you off on your own like this," he said. But Mrs. Toft persuaded him that Bridget would only be frightened if he came too.

"Is she going to come to live with us, Mummy?" asked Hilary as soon as they were walking along the street.

"If we can persuade her to."

"I think she wants to come, really, you know. She even said so once."

"All the same, I don't think it will be all that easy to persuade her. Do you know why she ran away?"

"Well, I know why she was going to run away before, but I thought she'd decided not to."

"Tell me about it."

Hilary never needed any encouragement to talk so she began to unfold the whole story. They walked along in the moonlight which was indeed almost as bright as day, though different. All the shadows were inky black and mysterious. Anything might be lurking in them. And there was no color; the moon turned everything it touched to silver. The streets were empty except for a few policemen on their beats. There was no traffic, until they got down to Holland Park Avenue, when a heavy lorry went hurtling past at about sixty miles an hour, making the sleeping streets reverberate.

At last they reached the broken wall in Holland Walk. "Here we are," said Hilary.

"So this is your secret."

"Yes. Do you think you can climb over?"

"I'll try."

They successfully clambered over, just in time to hear the tramp of a policeman's feet pass down the Walk when they were safely hidden.

"It is a garden," said Hilary in a hushed whisper. "It belongs to nobody, because nobody lives here. I don't know where she'll be in it. We can look in the likely places. I'll show you."

Mrs. Toft followed with the flashlight, flashing it in amongst the shrubs and ivy. There were strange little spat-

terings of silver moonlight filtering through the trees, but above one could see through the leaves the moon, yellow like a cheese and almost round, pared off a bit on one side. The yellow of the moon was the only color. Everything else was in blacks and greys and the touches of moonlight on the shiny ivy leaves were white and colorless. Only where the circle of light flashed into the shrubbery could one see the greens and the browns of leaf and earth—but no Bridget.

First they looked in the shed and the boiler house. Hilary went in softly mewing, and her mother followed flashing the light round the drifts of dead leaves. There was no one there. So they left the shrubbery through the door in the wall next to the greenhouse. This part of the garden was much lighter, and it seemed absurd to have the flashlight on. The place was all bathed in the moonlight. Nettles and apple trees, the yellow dandelions, scarlet poppies and the flowers they had planted, all wore an indistinctive grey, and the faintly sighing seas of pink willow herb were colorless. In this cold dead world Hilary was surprised to catch a whiff of scent from the last syringa; it seemed to belong to a world of colors.

They looked in the greenhouse and in the lairs. They searched the summerhouse and Hilary slithered through all the secret alleyways in the grass. But there was no Bridget. They combed the garden with the greatest care. Though scratched and stung they would not be deterred from penetrating to the farthest and most inaccessible corners. Yet more and more hopelessly they ranged up and down—Hilary softly mewing and listening for an answer, and Mrs. Toft swinging the beam of her flashlight round and peering after it to see a scarlet poppy suddenly revealed in color, but never what she sought. At last they paused by the edge of the shrubbery.

"I suppose she can't have come here. It's too obvious," said Hilary dejectedly.

Mrs. Toft made for the circle of seats round the urn and they both sat down, for they were exhausted.

"Do you think she could be in the house?"

"We never went into it before. I don't somehow think she would go there, but we ought to look."

"Yes, I suppose so." They both looked at the silent, lifeless pile of the bombed house, but neither made a move, until Hilary suggested, "We could have a biscuit, you know."

Mrs. Toft seemed to think that this would be a good idea so Hilary went off to fetch the tin. She returned excited. "She *has* been here," she whispered. "Look, there are no biscuits left."

NINETEEN

Flight and Refuge

That afternoon Bridget, as soon as she had been able to throw off Hilary after school, had gone up to the garden and fetched the biscuits. Then she went to the post office at the bottom of Ladbroke Grove and cashed a few savings stamps; they were sold in school on Fridays and occasionally she had bought one. Then she took a 52 bus to Victoria station.

It was her intention to go down into the country and get herself a job. "I can work very well on a farm or as a gardener," she thought. "I know a lot about these things, and I like it. It'll be much better if I can look after myself and not be dependent on anyone. Nobody wants me, so I shall go and earn my own living."

Of course she realized that people would think she was too young to do this; but then, she could make herself look older than she was. For this purpose she had purloined some lipstick and powder of her aunt's, and she had brought with her in her satchel one of her non-school dresses to change into. No one would employ a schoolgirl in uniform. They might guess she had run away. "But once I have got a job and established myself, then perhaps I'll tell my relations, or anyway write to Mrs. Toft. When they see that I've fixed myself up, they'll be very glad to have me off their hands and they won't fuss about my being too young." At this point she started to daydream and imagined Mrs. Toft and Hilary coming to visit her in the country. There she, as under-gardener—she preferred the idea of a garden to a farm—would show them the peas and beans and talk wisely about the roses and the herbaceous border, and Hilary would be horribly jealous of her grown-up status.

She had fixed on Lewes as her destination because she knew something of the country. She could remember from their walks various farms and gardens where she could inquire for employment.

The 52 bus had now reached the station yard and the passengers were crowding off it. Bridget followed in the tail of the crowd and crossed the yard and went into the booking hall, where she joined a queue for tickets. As it was a Friday evening the station was very crowded and long lines of weekenders were queueing for tickets. There were a couple of policemen in the booking hall and Bridget felt sure they had their eyes on her as she moved forward slowly in the queue. But surely Mrs. Sanders would not have noticed her absence yet.

At last her turn came, and she asked how much was a half ticket to Lewes. To her horror it cost more than her savings, so she asked how far she could go on them. The ticket man recommended that she should go by bus, but just then the old lady in the queue behind her, who had been listening to the conversation, interrupted with "Don't you worry, my dear. How much more do you need?" and started to bring some money out of her own purse. Before Bridget could refuse this kind offer, however, the old lady's son, a big burly man, had objected. "Why can't the child go by bus?" he demanded. "Why should we be expected to provide for her? She shouldn't be allowed to beg."

To this another member of the queue objected. "She never asked for nothing," he said.

The son felt bound to reply to this in round terms and a rumpus resulted. One of the policemen stepped up, but by the time he had got to the bottom of the matter the "child" had disappeared. The old lady was sorry, and would have liked to have made a search, but in this no one supported her.

Bridget had melted into the crowd. She did not take much notice of where she was going until she was well away from the scene, and then she stopped a moment to consider the situation. Obviously she had better take a bus. So, having asked the way, she set off for the bus station. This, she found, was not very far away. But to her horror it seemed to be swarming with policemen. Immediately she felt sure that her flight had been discovered, and that the policemen at the railway station had alerted the police at the bus station. They were on the look-out for her. So she walked on down the road trying to appear as if she had never intended to turn into the bus station.

What should she do now? "Well," she thought, "any place will do as well as Lewes. Why should I be so fixed on Lewes? I can go somewhere not so far away, somewhere that I can walk to." She did not realize that she would have to walk seven or eight miles out of the center of London before she would reach anything that faintly resembled country.

"Which way shall I go?" she thought. She was still walking steadily down the street, as she thought that would excite less notice than if she stood still to think. East, she decided would be no good. She would only reach the sea that way, for she knew that the River Thames flowed eastwards through London to the sea. South would be dangerous because Surrey and her other aunt were in that direction, and if she struck that district she would be known. Besides the police knew she had been making for Lewes, also to the south. North she knew nothing about, and to the west was Kew and Richmond. To go north, into the unknown, frightened her. On the whole she felt it would be better to go west.

"I must be walking west now," she thought, "so I shall go on in this direction."

When she had walked quickly for about three-quarters of an hour she was already beginning to feel how hard the pavements were, for walking in London is very much more tiring than walking in the country. She began to calculate how far she thought she had yet to go, measuring it by the memory of the trip to Kew on the 27 bus, and it seemed an intolerably long way.

"I shall wear my shoes out, and that will be no way to

start work. I think I shall have to catch a bus. After all, the police can't have their eyes on every bus in London." The road she was walking down had many buses going to and fro on it and so when she reached the next bus stop she examined the list of destinations, but unfortunately no buses went to Kew or Richmond. "Can I be walking in the wrong direction?" she thought. So she crossed the road and examined the bus stop on the other side, with no more success.

"Well, I suppose that Richmond buses just happen not to go along this road. The 27 route must have been rather to the north of this." Upon this she decided to strike north through the side streets.

Once you turn into the side streets of London, you fast lose your sense of direction. There is an intricate honeycomb of streets not quite at right angles to one another, varied with cul-de-sacs and crescents and roads which start off in one direction and then decide to turn round and go in another. Bridget walked and walked, but before long she had lost count of how many turns she had taken and no longer knew in what direction she was walking. When she came upon a busy main street she had an uncanny feeling that it was the same one that she had left in the first place. But as she had not noted the name then, she could not be sure.

She looked again at the numbers on the bus stop and at the list of destinations. No buses went to Richmond, and the more she looked at the numbers the less certain could she be that they were not the ones she had seen before. This uncertainty brought her near crying.

On the other side of the road stood a policeman. He

had seen Bridget consulting the bus stop and he noticed how miserable she looked. “That child has lost her way,” he thought.

Bridget saw the policeman coming towards her. Quickly, she turned and walked away. There was a side street. She turned down it and ran. But she must not be seen running—that would be suspicious—so she looked around to see if she were still followed. The policeman was not yet in sight, but might be at any moment. Where could she hide? She glanced round and found herself standing outside the doorway of a church, which was open, so she went in.

As the swing door of the porch closed to, the hubbub of the outside world was suddenly exchanged for the peaceful and harmonious strains of the organ. But as her eyes got used to the half-light Bridget realized that there was no congregation attending a service, as she had first feared. There was just the organist playing in the empty church, practising, perhaps. Much relieved Bridget slipped into a pew. She chose one where a pillar hid her from the organ.

How pleased she was to sit down! "I wonder how long I have been walking," she thought. "My feet are quite worn out. And I'm hungry too." So she felt in her pocket for the biscuits. "No one will see me eating them," she thought, looking round once more to make sure there was no one there. And there was no one.

She ate a biscuit, and she ate another, and the organist went on playing and nothing disturbed the peace of the church. "I have given that policeman the slip," thought Bridget, but no sooner had she thought this than the porch door creaked. "Oh, dear, that will be him!" she gasped to herself as she slipped under the pew.

It was not the policeman who came in, but an old lady.

Bridget soon recognized her mistake when she heard the shuffling, uncertain footsteps coming up the aisle. No policeman ever walked like that.

The old lady came slowly up the aisle and then she went into the pew directly behind Bridget's and knelt down. The pews were made with the backs going right down to the floor so that solid pine boards separated her knees from Bridget lying amongst the hassocks, and she could not see her at all. But Bridget distinctly heard the shuffling of her feeling for a hassock and the creaking of her bones as she lowered herself onto it, and her heavy breathing. Bridget held her own breath and lay as still as a stone monument, but it was very uncomfortable and cramped and extremely dusty. "I hope she doesn't pray long," she said to herself, "for I can scarcely rise out from under the pew before her very eyes. And I am going to sneeze."

It is practically impossible to suppress a sneeze entirely, though one can turn it into a sort of snort, as Bridget did on this occasion. It sounded terrible in the confined space under the pew. She could not but believe that even the organist would hear it and stop playing, and that the very dead might think it was the last trump and come out of their tombs. But nothing happened. The organist continued playing and the old lady continued her devotions.

"She must be very deaf," thought Bridget. Which probably was the explanation.

At last the old lady finished her prayers, and rose, creaking, to her feet. Bridget lay still in her place, waiting for her to leave the church. She had a long time to wait. First the old lady went and spoke to the organist. He did not stop playing to answer her but evidently she had a lot to say. Next the old lady went down to the back of the church and could be heard pottering about there, rearranging piles of hymnbooks and prayerbooks and dropping them and picking them up again. Then at last the door creaked, and the church was empty but for the organist and herself.

"Good," said Bridget and turned over and began to crawl out.

The church clock began to strike. She stopped. It would be as well to know the time.

The organist stopped playing. The clock finished striking. Eight.

"Later than I thought," said Bridget to herself.

The organist was moving about, closing up the organ, putting away his music and switching off the electricity which worked the pumps.

"He'll see me," she thought, and lay still. "I'll wait until he's gone."

She heard him walking briskly down the aisle, and then the swing door creaked. Then there was the groan of a heavier door, and the clang as it went to.

A horrible suspicion entered Bridget's head. "Oh dear," she said as she ran down the aisle. And she was right—she was locked in. "And they won't open it until morning, and I shall be found then and sent straight back to my aunt's. Oh, what can I do?" She looked hopelessly round the church at the narrow stained glass windows set high in the grey stone walls. They were well out of reach.

"I must just have a look round," she thought. But she did not hope for a way out. She was crying already and all her hopes seemed to have dissolved into thin air. All she could think of was, "I'm locked in," and, "They'll send me back to my aunt's."

Further down the church she found a door into the vestry, which seemed very dirty and forlorn. Part of it was curtained off with some old blackout curtains, and this was cleaner than the rest. White surplices hung here, and there was a table with a crucifix on it, and a small fireplace over which hung a photograph of the choir taken outside the main door of the church in July 1946. There was also a door beside the fireplace. This was not locked, and led into a small room beyond, where there was a washbasin with a water heater over it and some buckets and mops, and another door. This time it was clearly an outside door and Bridget saw with joy and relief that the key was in the lock. It was bolted also.

Bridget turned the key. Yes, it was all right. It worked. She turned it back again, and stood listening. Outside the door the street was busy with traffic and people walking past. She took the key out of the keyhole and put her eye to it. The key was large, and so the keyhole was large too, and she could see quite a lot of the street with people hurrying past, and cars and buses. On the opposite side was a cinema with a long queue of people moving slowly into the foyer, which was brightly lit, although, in the long summer evening, it was far from dusk. And there she saw what she feared to see—a policeman.

"Oh dear! He is sure to see me coming out. He will know no one should be coming out of this door at this hour and then he will recognize me and I shall be taken back to my aunt's." And the tears came again. To Bridget by now every policeman was on the lookout for her. Everything she did must be noticeable, and appear suspicious to them. She thought that they must all by now be furnished with her photograph and fingerprints and as soon as one set eyes on her she would be recognized and carried off.

And yet, it was only a little after eight, and her aunt had not yet informed the police that she was missing.

So she put the key back into the lock and stood crying. At length she wiped her eyes and blew her nose and thought, "Crying won't do you any good. He won't stay there forever. You'll just have to wait." And she went back into the church.

It was quiet and peaceful in there. The noise of traffic only came in as a distant hum, and did not disturb the stillness. A ray of light came in through the stained glass and made a splash of color on one of the grey pillars. She sat down just underneath it.

How safe she felt in there! No one knew she was there, no one could possibly guess she was there, no one could look in and see her, and no one would come in until tomorrow morning. "I shall have to get out before then," she thought, "but now I have the place to myself." And she began to feel sleepy.

"I have a long journey still before me," she thought. "Now is my opportunity to have a rest. I can sleep quite safely here."

She made a mattress of hassocks in the bottom of one of the pews where she was sheltered from the draught, and lay down and went to sleep.

TWENTY

Bridget Remembers

She woke up suddenly, cold and stiff. It was dark, very dark, she thought. Where was she? There was a light somewhere, flickering. And all at once she was back, in her mind, years back. She was up in a hayloft in Guernsey and the lamp that she saw was not the sanctuary lamp flickering before the altar, but a lantern in the barn below.

She could remember very clearly that night in Guernsey, although she had not thought about it since, although she had been determined not to think about it. And now that lamp flickering and herself lying hidden in the pew had brought it all back to her, and she could not help thinking about it. And as she thought, she realized that she had been thinking about it all the time, somewhere at the back of her mind, despite all her determination.

It had happened while she had been in hiding in the farm buildings at the Champignons, after the Germans had killed her mother. She had been sleeping in the hayloft, hidden, when suddenly she had been awakened by voices down below, and the lantern. And the voices were speaking in German. Her first thought had been, "They are looking for me!" and she had lain still without breathing. Then she realized that no one was looking for anyone. By turning her head slightly she could see them and they were sitting below on upturned boxes talking to one another. Between them was another box with a bottle and glasses on it.

"What on earth can they be doing here?" she wondered. "Two Germans?" One was in uniform and one was not. Just then the one who was not in uniform laughed, a kind of deep cackle which shook him through and through. It was a characteristic laugh; how well she knew it! It was Michel's laugh—Michel, Mrs. Champignon's eldest son.

"I didn't know he spoke German," she thought, not realizing what it meant.

He was nice, Michel, and she liked him. They had often met in the fields and chatted. He was the only one of the Champignons that she had talked to much. They had been talking together only a few days before, in fact, on the fatal day when they had taken her mother away. Michel had met her looking for mushrooms and had helped her to find some. Lying hidden in the hayloft she remembered how, when she had her basket full, she had urged him to have some of them and he had said, "Oh no, you keep them. We don't have to go out looking for mushrooms. We have plenty of them at home!" He had laughed, and she had laughed too. It was a good joke—the Champignons were a large family.

Then he had said, "That was a good speech Churchill made last night, wasn't it?" and she had said, "Oh, yes."

She had said, "Oh, yes," and had not thought about it at all. She had not spoken of it to her mother. And so as she lay stiffly above in the hayloft hearing Michel speak German to a German soldier, the pieces suddenly fell together and she realized what had happened. He spoke German and was friendly with the Germans. He had said to her, "That was a good speech Churchill made last night, wasn't it?" and she had said, "Oh, yes." So he knew they had a radio and were listening to English programs. He had found out from her idle "Oh, yes" that they had the forbidden radio and he had informed against them, to the Germans. Now the German soldier below was passing money across to Michel, and Michel was laughing. He had sold her mother. And she, Bridget, had betrayed her to him. She remembered it all so vividly that it was almost as though it had all happened over again, there in the empty church.

She stood up in the pew, white-faced and horrified. She had not allowed herself to think of the horror of it before. She had been determined not to think of it. She had been forced to live with the Champignons afterwards, knowing what Michel had done. Twice more she had run away, and would not tell anyone why. At last they had let her stay with some other neighbors. But the horrible knowledge had stayed in the back of her mind, rooted deep and not to be forgotten, the knowledge that her mother had been sold by Michel, whom she had known and liked, and that she, Bridget, had betrayed her to Michel with that "Oh, yes."

"No one shall ever know!" she cried out loud, and the flame of the sanctuary lamp quivered and flickered as if it heard and was horrified. "But I should like to tell Mrs. Toft," she said and sat down on the seat and sobbed.

At last she stopped sobbing and was quiet. Everything was quiet. The moonlight came silently in at the windows touching the tall pillars with silver. And the lamp burned steadily before the altar.

She got up and went out into the vestry, taking a chair with her to stand on to draw the upper bolt. She turned the key. The door opened easily and she went out into the street. She did not yet know where she intended to go, but she began to make her way northwest once more.

Anyone who knew the neat and tidy Bridget would hardly have recognized her in the dishevelled apparition which flitted from shadow to shadow. The moon had gone down and the night was very dark. Everywhere looked the same, endlessly the same. But Bridget had been so dazed by what she had remembered that she just wandered on, going nowhere.

At last she began to wonder where she was. "I should have stayed in the church," she thought. "I was safe there." Then she remembered how they would have come in the morning and found her and taken her back to her aunt's. "I'll never go back to my aunt's," she said.

She began to long for a landmark she could recognize. She was lost now, entirely lost. Ahead of her she could see the lights of a main road, for the side streets were unlit. "Perhaps I shall know the name of it," she thought. But when she reached the corner there was no name written up.

"I may be anywhere," she thought. "Just anywhere." And then gradually the street began to look familiar to her. Somewhere she had seen it before, though she could not tell where. Perhaps it was only in a dream. She stood there trying to capture the memory that escaped her. What did it remind her of? Had she actually seen this place or just somewhere rather like it? Where and when could it have been?

Then suddenly the memory came back to her and she knew. It was from the 27 bus that she had seen it. The bus had stopped a little way along this street to her left, and it was from there that Mrs. Toft had pointed out to her Holland Park and the deserted gardens. She felt no doubt that it was the same place.

It was very sweet to feel the relief of knowing where she was. She did not think twice. She had no doubt now where she was going. The secret garden was like home to her. Perhaps tomorrow Hilary would come, and oh! perhaps she would say that Mrs. Toft wanted her to come and live with them.

"How silly of me to think that," Bridget said to herself immediately, "when I know that they won't want me. But tomorrow I can catch a 27 bus and go to Richmond."

The only problem was to cross the floodlit expanse of road before her, for, if anyone were about, she would be sure to be seen and stopped. Just as she was wondering if she could safely do it, she heard the measured tread of a policeman echoing in the emptiness. He was a long way off as yet, but coming towards her, so that he would see her as soon as she started out on to the lighted roadway. It was hopeless to go then, so she pressed herself back into the shadow of a doorway, and listened to his footsteps coming nearer and nearer. With luck, he would not see her where she was.

He passed her and went on. She watched his back until he was about a hundred yards away and then she took her chance, with a headlong rush across the lighted road into the shelter of a dark archway opposite. There she stood gasping back her breath, pressed against the wall. When she dared to peep out the policeman was still walking away along his beat.

When she had gathered breath and was calm again, she came out from the archway and slipped along the wall. She must find some turning up from the main road here which would take her up the hill towards the garden. Presently such a turning came and there was the name written up that she had been hoping for—Holland Walk. She had not been mistaken. Here was the other end of the familiar lane. Gratefully she ran up into the pitchy darkness, up the gently sloping side of Campden Hill and over the crest to where the broken wall was—and in she leapt. Never had she been so agile before. It was like leaping into bed when one is tired.

There it all was—the ivy catching at her feet and the slight scent of the syringa, the soft earth instead of hard paving stones, the familiar, instead of the strange. She breathed and waited, watching the dark outline of the trees against the dark sky and listening for the faint garden noises in the silence. Then something caught her listening ear—movement and voices from the house. She swung round. There was a light. And she could see people moving, how many she could not say, but more than one. And one was small, a child in fact. It would be Hilary and the police. Hilary, too, was a traitor.

TWENTY ONE

Home at Last

Hilary and her mother were just emerging from the house. Mrs. Toft had been unwilling to search the place properly. "No, don't, dear, it's dangerous," she had said over and over again. "We can't see where there are holes in the dark. Or anything might give way. No, dear, don't, I say. You might break your neck."

"All right, I won't," said Hilary. "I don't suppose she's in here, anyway. We never used to come in here."

"Let's go, then. This place is horribly dangerous. Give me the flashlight. You go first."

Hilary went out first, but in a moment she was back clutching at her mother's arm, whispering breathlessly—"There's someone just come into the garden—someone's moving—I heard—I saw—it's her!"

"Where?"

But Hilary had gone, rushing ahead, waving her arms and shouting as loud as she dared, "It's me! It's Hilary!"

And Mrs. Toft followed as eagerly, but more sedately. Presently Hilary was at her side again, crestfallen.

"She ran away. I can't find her."

"Are you sure you saw her?"

"Yes, I saw her running away from me."

"Are you sure it was Bridget?"

"Yes. Yes, I know it was Bridget. Why should she run away?"

"Did she go out of the garden?"

"No, she ran into it."

"Quick, Hilary, go to the gap in the wall and stay there. There's no other way out, is there?"

"There's none that we know of."

"Right. I'll go and look for her."

"Mayn't I look for her?"

"No, you go and guard the way out. We mustn't let her slip through our fingers. Quick, dear!"

Mrs. Toft wanted to find Bridget herself so that she could be the first to ask her to come and live with them; otherwise Bridget would never believe that she was really wanted. When Hilary had gone to the gap in the wall, Mrs. Toft went out on to the lawn and stood there thinking. Where would she hide if she were Bridget? She knew the garden fairly well now as she had combed it several times in their unsuccessful search. There were the lairs under the apple trees. But no, she would not hide there—that was the first place where Hilary would look. Somewhere where the nettles and undergrowth were uncut—would she rush in and sting herself rather than be found? Or the summerhouse? Perhaps behind the summerhouse?

But no. She remembered the old boiler house piled high with leaves inside. That was where she would go. So she went there, and went in with the flashlight in her hand. There was nothing to be seen but leaves, leaves and leaves. Could Bridget be hidden under them? Mrs. Toft switched off the light and stood listening. There was nothing at first save her own heartbeat and breathing. Then she heard another noise, the quiet breathing of another person in there amongst the leaves.

"Bridget, it is me, Mrs. Toft."

And she felt among the leaves where she heard the breathing and found a body and an arm and felt the pulse racing with terror.

"It is only Mrs. Toft. Is it you, Bridget?"

"Are the police with you?"

"No, I am alone. And Hilary is by the gap in the wall. We came to find you."

"You didn't bring the police?"

"No. Surely you trust Hilary. She wouldn't tell the police a thing when they questioned her. She would not betray you. You must trust people more, Bridget. You think all the world's against you, but they're not. There are those who would do anything rather than you should come to harm. I would. Please trust us."

And Bridget burst out, "How can I trust people when—" It was all in her mind but she did not know how to tell it.

"When what?" asked Mrs. Toft quietly.

"I betrayed my own mother." And then she told her what she had remembered in the church. Mrs. Toft listened without interrupting. And when it was told, Bridget felt unbelievably relieved.

"But what do you mean, you betrayed your mother?" said Mrs. Toft. "You didn't betray your mother at all. Has that been worrying you all this time? It was Michel who betrayed her."

"But I—"

"I know you said, 'Oh, yes'," interrupted Mrs. Toft. "But that was an accident. You never dreamt of betraying her. Michel was very clever. He *led* you into saying that. And, you know, I think he would have found out somehow without that."

"Do you think so?"

"I'm sure. Now promise me one thing, Bridget."

"What?"

Bridget thought that she would ask her not to run away again, but instead she said, "To remember that you did not betray your mother."

"Oh!" Bridget was surprised because she felt very happy all of a sudden, as if a weight had been lifted off her mind. Then she added, "Yes."

"And now," said Mrs. Toft, "will you come and live with us?"

Just then Hilary appeared. She had tired of waiting by the wall and could no longer hear her mother moving about in the garden. She had sensed that Bridget was found, and leaving her post she heard voices as she passed the boiler house and came in, all eager and excited.

"Here you are, here you are!" she cried. "You do look a sight!" For Mrs. Toft had turned the flashlight on again when Hilary came in and they both saw what a mess Bridget was in. There were leaves in her hair and her clothes were crumpled and dusty. "Why did you hide from us? I called out that it was me."

"I thought you had the police with you."

"Oh no, there was only us. You didn't think we'd bring the police, did you, not really? We wouldn't send them to search you out, not for worlds."

Mrs. Toft asked her question again, before Hilary could bring it up. "You will come and live with us now, won't you?"

Bridget said, "You don't really want me."

"Oh, Bridget, I have been thinking of it for a long time," said Mrs. Toft, "and I only hesitated because I didn't know if *you* would want to come. . . ."

"Oh yes, I want to!" burst out Bridget, and then added, "That is, if you really want me."

"And of course we do," said Mrs. Toft.

"Of course we do. You know we do," Hilary insisted.

It was still night when they left the garden and nothing could be seen but the stars in the sky above. But as they climbed Ladbroke Grove, suddenly Bridget said, "Listen, the birds are singing!"

And as they stopped to listen they looked up into the sky and saw little clouds floating in it like curdled milk, all incandescent with the first light. And as they went on, the morning light spread pale and chilly, but hopeful. Hilary thought it must be about breakfast time, but when they got home she found it was only a quarter to four.